"So you never mix business with pleasure?"

He brushed her hand off his shoulder. "I don't mix pleasure and you."

He really was cute when he was annoyed. No wonder she'd gotten such a kick out of pestering him as a kid. She placed her hand on his bare knee, enjoyed the feel of his muscles tensing.

Jack swore. "Haven't you ever heard that *no* means *no?*"

Piper laughed. "No only means *no* when the woman says it."

"That's sexist," he complained. "I care about you, Pest. We grew up together."

So this was his excuse? He still thought she was a kid? She let her voice go husky. "I'm all grown up now." She shimmied just a little in her seat. "Or ...en't you noticed?"

Dear Reader,

Saving the Girl Next Door is the third book in my HEROES INC. miniseries. After stranding my characters in *Daddy to the Rescue* (HI #705, 4/03) in the mountains, and writing a book in the heart of New York City in *Defending the Heiress* (HI #709, 5/03), I was ready to move south to the sultry tropical heat of Florida.

When I started writing about Piper Payne and Jack Donovan, I knew this would be a special book. The characters wouldn't stop talking to me. Piper and Jack took on a life of their own. The story is hot and sassy and the suspense cutting edge. But best of all, the story is fun.

Harlequin is so pleased with the HEROES INC. miniseries that more of these books will be coming your way next year. I hope you enjoy my efforts, and I always love hearing from readers, so please feel free to stop by my Web site and visit at www.SusanKearney.com.

Susan Kearney

SAVING THE GIRL NEXT DOOR

SUSAN KEARNEY

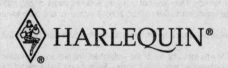

TORONTO • NEW YORK • LONDON
AMSTERDAM • PARIS • SYDNEY • HAMBURG
STOCKHOLM • ATHENS • TOKYO • MILAN • MADRID
PRAGUE • WARSAW • BUDAPEST • AUCKLAND

ISBN 0-373-22713-2

SAVING THE GIRL NEXT DOOR

Copyright © 2003 by Susan Hope Kearney

Visit us at www.eHarlequin.com

Printed in U.S.A.

ABOUT THE AUTHOR

Susan Kearney used to set herself on fire four times a day. Now she does something really hot—she writes romantic suspense. While she no longer performs her signature fire dive (she's taken up figure skating), she never runs out of ideas for characters and plots. A business graduate from the University of Michigan, Susan is working on her next novel and writes full-time. She resides in a small town outside Tampa, Florida, with her husband and children and a spoiled Boston terrier. Visit her at http://www.SusanKearney.com.

Books by Susan Kearney

HARLEQUIN INTRIGUE

CLASSIFIED

For Your Information.
Read and Destroy:

The SHEY GROUP is a private paramilitary organization whose purpose is to take on high-risk, high-stakes missions in accord with U.S. government policy. All members are former CIA, FBI or military with top-level clearances and specialized skills. Members maintain close ties to the intelligence community and conduct high-level behind-the-scenes operations for the government as well as for private individuals and corporations.

The U.S. government will deny any connection with this group.

Employ at your own risk.

CAST OF CHARACTERS

Jack Donovan—The highly trained daredevil pilot and Shey Group operative is willing to assist the girl who used to live next door. However, helping Piper Payne will require him to place both his life and his heart in jeopardy.

Piper Payne—A good cop who has been framed and fired, she needs Jack's help to clear her name. She's also set on losing her virginity to her former teenage crush.

Vince Edwards and Leroy James—These two ordinary citizens have accused Piper of taking bribes—and nearly destroyed her career.

Aaron Hodges—A brilliant, eccentric computer entrepreneur. When questioned, he's openly hostile, but does that make him guilty?

Danna Mudd—Hacker extraordinaire, she possesses the talent to pull off a crime, and the social skills to cast suspicion elsewhere.

John Smith, aka Easy As Pie—He's big, dangerous and deceptive, but does he have the brains to set up Piper?

Venus De Lux—A wealthy hooker with a fond attachment to the wrong kind of man.

For Patricia Smith, an editor whose wise guidance is much appreciated. Thanks, Patricia!

Prologue

The cop wouldn't be sticking her nose where it didn't belong, not anymore, not after some intensely smooth computer hacking. Thanks to a back door in the police department's computer program and two "solid citizens" who'd come forward and accused her of taking a bribe, detective Piper Payne had had her chain yanked good and tight.

She'd better get used to being out of the loop. Hung out to dry.

But just in case she persisted in her annoying inquiry, she now had bugs on her phone, worms on her computer and a miniature tracking and listening device in her wallet. She would be watched.

And if she made another wrong move, the chain would tighten around her neck. She wouldn't just lose her job, she'd lose her life.

Chapter One

Jack Donovan had a reputation for attaining success—even if it required dive-bombing his chopper through a hailstorm of bullets. Today no one was shooting at him, but if he'd known what waited for him down below, he might never have landed.

When he was a Navy SEAL, Jack had scuba dived five oceans and climbed mountains on four continents. Nevertheless, with his instinctive timing and superb reflexes, he'd been born to fly. For the military he'd flown test aircraft, and for his current employer, the Shey Group, he flew everything from gliders to jets to helicopters.

Blissfully unaware of his fate, Jack couldn't have ordered a better day for flying the chopper. The Florida sky above the Gulf of Mexico shimmered a rich silky blue that was full of promise. With not even a hint of a thundercloud in sight, Jack cruised above Clearwater's sandy shoreline with no more on his mind than his anticipation of landing smoothly, then kicking back with an icy brew in a honky-tonk bar along the beach, where he could watch the sun set over the Gulf.

He sighted his landing field. At one thousand feet above his target, Jack powered down his engines. Man and machine plummeted toward the earth. If he had been in a plane, he'd have had to dive the nose down to pick up enough speed to glide. But in a chopper, he maneuvered his hands and feet to autorotate the rotors, a basic landing maneuver that every pilot practiced in case the engines conked out during a flight.

Without his heart even skipping a beat, Jack lightly touched down and abandoned one dream vehicle for another, his latest acquisition, a new Mercedes coupe. He chose his cars like his women—fast and sleek and ready to run. After striding across the tarmac to his silver convertible, which had sat all afternoon in the baking sun, he slid behind the wheel. The leather seat was hot enough to make him wince.

He'd forgotten how extreme a Florida summer could be. Although Jack had grown up in Clearwater, he hadn't been back home in years.

Bad memories of fights with his parents during his wild and reckless teenage years had kept him away. A decade ago Clearwater hadn't been a big enough town for Jack Donovan. Except for spring break when college students flocked to the community's tacky souvenir shops and powder sand beaches, the sleepy beachside town wasn't a happening place.

Jack turned on the radio and air conditioner full blast. As Black Sabbath blared from his speakers, he pressed a button that caused the Mercedes' hardtop to automatically fold into the trunk.

Yes, baby. Wind and sun and surf, here I come.

Years ago Jack had yearned for Paris, Tahiti and Nepal, and the navy had given him the means to fulfill his dreams. He'd since circumnavigated the world by boat and plane more times than he could count. The navy had also given him the discipline to turn himself into a productive citizen.

Now he was employed by the Shey Group, a private team of men, formerly with the military or one of the intelligence agencies, who charged high fees to take on missions that required special skills and classified connections. Working for the Shey Group allowed him the luxury of this silver coupe with its souped-up engine that could go from zero to sixty in 4.6 seconds. Not to mention his friends, the elite of the elite. Good guys to have at his side in a brawl. Not that Jack anticipated a fight. Not while on vacation.

Whistling, contented, he burned rubber, exiting the private airport. The car handled like the high-priced luxury item that she was, and he headed for the beach.

A cute yellow VW Bug pulled out behind him.

At the next corner Jack turned right. So did the yellow VW.

He might be on vacation, but Jack's normal observation skills kicked in. That's why he could take so many chances and still have all his body parts—he took *calculated* risks. Just for the hell of it, he made two right turns and then another left.

The VW Bug stuck to him like a flea.

Dark tinted windows prevented him from identifying the driver. But Jack no longer had any doubts that someone was following him. He had several choices. Since the Volkswagen could never match his speed, he could accelerate and lose the tail. Or he could confront his pursuer and find out what the hell was going on.

Intel first. With a grin of pleasure Jack pressed his foot down on the accelerator, hard, but not enough to outrun the VW.

The car matched his speed. The other driver was determined, but kept a constant distance between them.

He sped through a green light and headed for the highway. The car stayed right with him.

Impressive. The driver of the other car didn't come too close, and yet Jack couldn't shake him, not without a flat-out race on the interstate. Exciting perhaps, and a choice he might have made as little as five years ago, but—no matter how much he wanted to stomp the pedal to the metal—he couldn't justify the risk to civilians.

However, now that he had some idea he might be dealing with a professional, he thought back over his past few missions. All of them had been sewed up tight. Logan Kincaid, his boss, didn't leave loose ends. But perhaps one of the team was working a case that he hadn't been brought up to speed on yet. A case that might be casting danger in his direction.

Jack turned down the heavy metal blaring from the radio and hit the call button of his cell phone.

"The Shey Group," a secretary answered.

"Logan Kincaid, please."

"Bored with your vacation, Jack?" Logan's warmly modulated voice came over the speaker phone.

His boss might not be in his office, but he was usually available. Using state-of-the-art technology, Logan had his calls forwarded to his cell phone so he could be reached 24/7, pretty much anywhere in the world. "Ready to take on your next assignment?"

"Sheesh. I just got here."

"So you aren't calling because you missed us already? What's up?"

"I called to ask you the same question."

"I don't understand."

"Any operations working that I should know about?"

"We're practically shut down."

"Then there's no reason for someone to be tailing me?"

"Jack, you haven't been down there twenty-four hours and you already have some jealous—"

"I haven't even checked in to a hotel." *Yet.* "I spent last night with my folks." A tense awkward evening he'd prefer to forget. How could they have raised a child and then have nothing to say to him except to criticize? In short order they'd disparaged his career. His friends. His lack of a family. His wheels. And his haircut. You'd have thought he had come home with five earrings and a tattoo, instead of this sweet little coupe.

"Don't your folks turn in around eleven?"

Logan never forgot a detail. He'd once overheard Jack calling his mother to wish her a happy birthday. She hadn't been pleased when Jack had roused her out of a sound sleep at 10:30 p.m. And Logan knew that Jack was a night owl and hadn't gone to sleep before midnight since he'd started shaving. So no doubt Logan thought he'd been out partying and had taken someone else's honey home and the car following was a jealous lover—but it wasn't like that.

"You need any help?" Logan offered.

If Jack asked, his boss would mobilize a team within twenty minutes. Jack lived for that kind of loyalty—something his parents wouldn't ever comprehend.

"I can handle it."

"You sure?"

"Yeah. I hardly think a yellow VW Bug would be the choice of an assassin."

He rechecked the side mirror. The car was still following him.

"Fine. Try not to get any speeding tickets."

Jack chuckled and let his foot ease off the gas. Just because he had superior reflexes and could handle high-speed maneuvers didn't mean the local cops would appreciate his breaking the law.

For the moment he adhered to the speed limit and allowed the tail to come after him. During his stint in the military Jack had learned the value of planning. He would pick the time and place for the confrontation with his mysterious pursuer. Someplace private. Where there was no chance of innocents catching a stray bullet.

Jack leaned over and opened the glove compartment. Driving with one hand, keeping his attention on the road, he reached for his gun. He tucked the weapon into the front of his jeans and checked the rearview mirror.

Soon. He would make his move.

Jack veered from the highway to the off-ramp. Two miles farther, he turned into an industrial section of town. He passed several rough-looking bars and crossed a parking lot to a dilapidated warehouse that squatted beside a chain-link fence overgrown with chin-high weeds. The doors of the warehouse had long since been scrapped, leaving him a dark, private spot in which to corner his pursuer.

Jack stepped on the gas, heading straight for the doorless entrance. He entered the building, jammed on the brakes and hauled on the wheel, whipping the car around until he faced the entrance.

Within seconds he'd exited his vehicle and taken cover in the shadows by the opening. He flicked off the gun's safety and aimed. Timing was critical.

The VW slowed, then halted just outside in the sunlight.

Come to me.

Just a little more.

The driver flicked on the headlights, and Jack averted his eyes to avoid being momentarily blinded. The car edged forward.

While the sight of his car distracted the driver, Jack lunged toward the Bug and the driver's door. He yanked on the handle. Employing several smooth moves, he pressed the gun to the driver's temple, locked his free arm around her throat and dragged her from the car.

A woman. Too surprised to resist?

Her hair was auburn, the fragrance scented by sunshine. Jack had yet to see her face, but bad people came in curvy shapes and 110-pound packages. With her back pressed to his chest, he couldn't mistake the hard bulge of her harness and gun poking his ribs.

The female was armed.

"Don't move one freakin' finger. Don't so much as breathe hard, sugar."

Odd. She still hadn't tensed. Didn't fight him.

Instead, she chuckled. "Oh, Jack. You always were such a hothead. You going to pat me down?"

He hadn't heard that voice in ten years. Two things became clear. She wasn't scared, but amused. And Jack immediately recognized her voice. "Piper?"

His next-door neighbor? The bane of his childhood existence? The pesky kid who had found his stash of *Playboy* magazines under his bed when he was nine? The tomboy who'd followed him all through his teenage years? The same Piper who'd spied on him while he got to second base with some cheerleader whose name he'd long since forgotten? The same Piper who had begged him for a ride on his motorcycle and then wouldn't go until he found her a helmet and promised not to speed?

Stifling a curse, Jack flicked his thumb to engage the gun's safety, then tucked the weapon into the small of his back. "Piper…Payne?"

She giggled. "In the flesh." He released her, but she didn't step away. Instead she turned to face him.

He had only a second to glimpse ivory skin and wide-set, mischievous eyes before she slipped her arms around his neck and bussed him right on the lips.

"Hey!" He stepped back.

And took a good look at her. He hadn't seen her since she was a skinny fifteen-year-old with braces and tattered jeans. The braces were gone, and she now boasted straight white teeth, full lips and a short nose dusted with freckles. She'd done something to her carrot-red hair, and it now shimmered a rich auburn with golden highlights. The same cool green eyes that he remembered stared back at him, her amusement mocking him.

She wore a skimpy white top that skimmed the curves of her breasts. No bra. If he stared hard enough, he might just make out the outline of her… *Hell!* This was Piper the Pest with a capital *P*. He wasn't going to leer at her chest, no matter how alluringly she dressed or didn't dress. He wasn't going to look at her bare midriff or the way her hips flared into her shorts. He certainly wasn't going to look at her long, tanned legs. And he most certainly wasn't going to think about her full breasts pressing against his chest or her kissing him.

He narrowed his eyes. "You were following me."

She shrugged a delicate shoulder and one of the thin straps of her top slid down her arm. "I'm so busted."

Piper had always known how to get under his skin. Always knew how to say the most irritating things.

Jack fought the urge to push the strap back where it belonged, and instead folded his arms over his chest. "Why were you following me?"

"I wanted to see you."

Obviously. When she avoided a direct answer to his question, his pulse rate shot up. Simply an excess of adrenaline. Surely she still couldn't be such an impossibly irritating brat, could she?

She raised her hands innocently. "What?"

Already she had him speaking through gritted teeth. "Why did you want to see me?"

"Your mom told me you were back, and I thought you might take me up for a ride. I arrived to see your engines fail and you dropping out of the sky like a dead duck." She flung her arms around his neck. And brushed his mouth with hers again. "I thought you were a goner."

"Nope."

She retreated half a step before he figured out how to react to her second kiss. She meant nothing by it. She'd always been as friendly as a stray puppy.

But his body wasn't reacting as if her hug was simply friendly. And his mind was stunned, his brain temporarily off-kilter, no doubt due to the fact that his circulatory system had erroneously sent all his blood to anatomical regions below his belt.

Down, boy. This one's not for you.

She scowled at him. "I should have known you were simply pulling some fool stunt."

"You were worried about me?"

Piper rolled her eyes. "I sure would have hated to see all that pretty machinery crash and burn."

She still hadn't told him the real reason she wanted to see him. The stubborn girl had grown into a stubborn woman. And she was all woman.

You shouldn't even look at her that way, Jack.

Even if she hadn't been the most annoying girl-child on the planet, even if she had grown into a woman who could knock his socks off, even if she was still single, the Pest and Jack Donovan together would never happen. They were like a Cuban sandwich with corned beef—they didn't mix well. Try to lump them together and they both got indigestion.

By-the-book Piper was a straight arrow. She'd never cheated in school. Never lied to her parents. Always came in by curfew. Didn't drive over the speed limit or run yellow lights. He'd bet a month's pay she hadn't tasted alcohol until she'd turned twenty-one.

He'd heard she'd become a cop, and he could imagine her writing tickets for jaywalking. Piper saw things in black and white, right and wrong, good and evil. For her there were no gray areas and no moral dilemmas. She was one of the few genuinely good people he knew—probably why he found her so damn exasperating.

Nope, she wasn't for him.

After last night's disaster with his parents, he had promised himself he would move into a hotel on the beach and spend the remaining days of his vacation with a warm, willing babe who wanted nothing from him except a good time. He should go home and pack.

However, if he did, he'd miss the sunset.

"How about a beer and a grouper sandwich?" he asked.

PIPER PAYNE HAD HAD a crush on Jack Donovan from the moment she'd first seen him twenty years ago. At age five, she hadn't known it was a crush—she'd just known the boy next door was really, really cool. He rode his two-wheeler bike faster than cars drove down their neighborhood street. He'd mastered skateboarding with barely a skinned knee. He climbed the huge granddaddy oaks in the backyard as fearlessly as any squirrel, but most amazing of all, he didn't care what anybody thought of him.

Piper had never met anyone as wild or self-sufficient as Jack. In turn he'd shocked, amazed and fascinated her with his daring stunts and reckless behavior. And no matter how often his parents or teachers punished him, his irrepressible spirit could not be squashed.

He never seemed to study. He rarely did his homework, but usually passed by acing his exams. A star athlete, he played soccer and basketball and was on the swim team. Other guys idolized him and girls started calling him for dates when he was twelve. She'd thought the girls were silly and the guys dumb.

Piper's parents had taught her to take satisfaction in working hard and achieving success. And, in turn, she took pleasure in pleasing authority figures. Following the rules was easy for her—a good thing, since her mother, who was a cop, and her father, a computer science professor at a nearby college, didn't miss much. She'd liked the praise that came with being told that she was a good kid and a model student. There was nothing wrong in growing up responsible. Nothing cool about drinking and driving or having sex in the back of your parents' minivan.

Still, she vividly recalled the day Jack had left home. The day he'd turned eighteen, his mother had neatly packed up his belongings, set them on the front porch and told him to leave. Defiant, Jack had spun off on his Harley, leaving the packed bags behind. She'd heard later that he had joined the navy, then some kind of high-tech paramilitary group, and over the years she'd occasionally wondered if he would ever come home.

His timing couldn't have been better. Who would have thought she'd ever need Jack Donovan's help?

Piper had majored in criminal justice at the University of South Florida. Following in her mother's footsteps, she'd attended the police academy and become a police officer. Six months ago she'd made detective.

Until recently, the only deficiency in her life, her only failure, was not finding the right man. She'd had a teenage crush on Jack and had once thought she'd lose her virginity to him. He'd been the coolest guy in town. A bad boy. Forbidden. But he'd left town before she was ready. And later not many guys were interested in a cop. But she couldn't blame her single status solely on her career choice. Even in college she'd had higher standards than most women. As a result she was still a virgin.

A twenty-five-year-old virgin with a ruined reputation. The irony wasn't lost on her. If she hadn't been so angry, she might have cried. She'd worked too hard to make detective to give up her career without a fight. She might be despondent, but no way was she ready to eat her .38. However, she didn't know how to track an enemy without one lead.

The people she'd counted on to help her in the past were her police family. Thanks to her being fired over the false charges against her, she could no longer go to them. She needed someone she could trust. Her feelings toward Jack were complex and unexpected. She was beginning to realize that she wanted more than his help—she wanted the comfort of his arms around her. But first things first. She had to tell him about her problem.

The Pelican Shack was frequented by the locals. Known for its grouper sandwiches, fresh oysters on the half shell and icy beer, the restaurant also boasted a fabulous view of beach, Gulf and spectacular sunsets. The sky, slices of orange and patches of purple, framed a huge orange sun dipping into the sea.

Their conversation had been awkward and sporadic. Stops and starts about the weather, the changes in the city, including the increased traffic and the brand-new roundabout the city was about to demolish, but nothing personal. When she'd set out to find Jack, asking him for help had seemed like a good plan. But now she realized that asking for his assistance was harder than she'd thought it would be.

Jack paid the bill, leaving the waitress a ten-dollar tip. In some ways he was the same old Jack, full of flash and hard to nail down. And yet she sensed, she fervently hoped, that with the years had come maturity. The old Jack would have demanded—before he'd ordered dinner—to know why she'd tracked him down. The new Jack had learned patience—either that or he simply didn't care one way or the other. He was still hard to read, keeping his thoughts close and his feelings closer.

She'd blown her opportunity to bring up her plea for help during dinner.

"How about a walk on the beach?" she suggested.

"There's no place you have to be? No one waiting for you?"

When she shook her head, he politely took her elbow as she stood. That was new, too. This new Jack had manners, polish. He was no longer the teenage boy who'd tickled her until she'd gone home in a huff, no longer the boy who was so skinny he needed a belt to hold up his jeans.

Age had made him more handsome. The tiny lines around his eyes added charm. His years with the SEALs had broadened his chest, but his hips were almost as narrow, his jeans tighter than tight. And his dark blue eyes reflected the integrity, courage and honor that she recognized from her work as a cop.

Almost satisfied that she'd found the right man to ask for help, she now had the task of getting out the actual words. Where to start?

Just say it.

With the sun setting, many beachgoers headed indoors, leaving them almost alone on the beach where the powder-white sand was some of the finest in the world. She and Jack strolled along in relative privacy and silence.

Ask him. He can only say no, and she'd be no worse off than she was right now.

She'd saved a few pieces of her roll, and she tossed them to the seagulls.

"Jack?"

"Yeah?"

"I tracked you down because—"

"I've always wanted to do that."

"Feed the seagulls?"

"Look." He pointed to a kid on a surfboard. Only, the kid wasn't surfing—not exactly. He wasn't relying on the waves for his momentum, but on an odd-shaped kite attached to a towrope. Pulled by the kite and wind, the kid was surfing toward the beach at about thirty miles an hour. And when the wind gusted, boy and surfboard soared into the air.

She tossed the last of her bread to the birds. He must be a fanatic to still be out on the water after sunset. While she estimated that he had another forty-five minutes of light before darkness set in, everyone else had left the water. "Looks like a great way to break your neck."

"Wow." Jack halted, his expression filled with fascination and delight. The kid performed some kind of daredevil aerial maneuver, then shot toward the beach. She should have known Jack couldn't resist anything fast and dangerous.

Maybe he hadn't found that maturity after all. In one afternoon he'd turned off the engine of his chopper and could have crashed, he'd sped down the highway like a race-car driver and he'd put a gun to her head—not exactly the actions of a mature and responsible man. Perhaps she'd made a mistake in thinking Jack could or would help her, and she no longer regretted her hesitation.

But he hadn't totally forgotten her. He stared at the kite surfer, but spoke to her. "Was there something you wanted to ask me?"

"Never mind."

There was no point in talking to the guy when he was so clearly captivated by a potential toy.

"You sure?"

"Yeah." She'd solve her own problem. Somehow.

Jack kicked off his shoes and waded into the surf. As the kid reeled in his kite, Jack snagged the surfboard and struck up a conversation. "I've surfed and wind sailed but I've never—"

"You want to try?" The kid stopped winding in the kite's rope.

She should never have put all her hopes in Jack helping her. She'd been wrong about him, only imagining a new maturity. He was as eager to try that kite-flying surfboard as a kid with a new toy.

Jack was already taking off his shirt and tossing it on the beach when he hesitated, glanced at her over his shoulder. "You sure there wasn't something you wanted to ask me?"

She shooed him on. "Go fly your kite, Jack."

Chapter Two

Jack had lost track of time while he'd learned how to kite surf. The timing was tricky, but the airborne freedom had been glorious. When he finally dragged himself back to the beach almost an hour later, Piper was gone.

He refused to feel guilty. It wasn't as if he'd asked her on a date and abandoned her. Yet curiosity gnawed at him.

Why had she tracked him down?

She could have told him over dinner. She'd had a chance to speak her mind then. Or she could have waited on the beach for him....

As Jack pulled into his parents' driveway, he glanced next door—just in time to see a flash of red hair before Piper turned out a light on the second story. A bedroom light? He couldn't be sure. Her folks' house had burned to the ground about a year ago, and they'd rebuilt, so the layout was unfamiliar.

What was she doing living with her parents?

He shouldn't be wondering about Piper. He should

go inside, pack and move to the hotel. Forget he'd run into her. Forget she'd kissed him. Twice. Forget how terrific she'd felt in his arms.

Not all of his memories of Piper were bad. At age fourteen, when he'd broken an arm and leg after crashing his minibike, he'd come home from the hospital expecting to find his precious bike long gone. But Piper had liberated his bike from the Dumpster where his father had tossed it, carefully saved all the parts and hidden it in her garage.

That didn't mean he owed her.

He also recalled a scrumptious meal of doughnuts that she'd smuggled to him after his folks had sent him to bed without dinner for stealing the family car to take a joyride. He'd been ten.

She wasn't all Pest.

He stared at the upstairs window, wishing he had his nightscope binoculars. Was she staring back at him?

Why couldn't he shake the connection? Almost as if she'd shot out a spiderweb to draw him to her, he had the strongest compulsion to join her.

Disgusted by the fact that he couldn't seem to ignore her, couldn't get her out of his mind, he hesitated. Piper might be all grown up, but he still thought of her as a kid. Yet no kid had such lush curves, and he was no good at applying the brakes—a dangerous combination. He should stay away. But she'd started to ask him something just before he'd gotten caught up in the kite surfing.

So what?

Just pack. Head for the beach. He didn't need any complications to spoil his vacation.

Jack wrung out his wet shirt and slung it over his shoulder. Ten minutes and he could be gone.

So why were his feet taking him across the yard toward the Payne house? He'd climb the old oak tree, just look in her window and make sure she was okay. Then he would go.

He kicked off his shoes, preferring to ascend with bare feet. Hand over hand, Jack pulled himself up until he was even with the second story. Massive branches easily supported his weight. He reached the room where he'd seen her, tried to peer inside.

And couldn't see a blasted thing.

Compelled to make sure she was okay, he lifted the window sash and climbed over the ledge. At the click of a gun's hammer cocking, he halted—half in, half out of the window.

He spoke softly. "It's me. Jack."

She flicked on a lamp, filling the room with a soft golden glow. "Is there something wrong with our front door?"

"Piper." Her mother called from down the hall. "Who are you talking to—"

"I'm fine, Mom. Go back to sleep." Piper set the gun on her dresser and then shut her door. "Mom's a light sleeper."

Jack finished climbing inside and closed the window. "You're still up?"

"Duh." She wore a white T-shirt that stopped at midthigh and showed off her tanned legs. She grabbed a robe and wrapped it around her, then belted it tight. "What are you doing here?"

He had no idea.

But he didn't want to leave. The room smelled like Piper, fresh and clean with a hint of feminine musk. And it was full of girly things—her purse on her dresser, a picture frame of her and her parents with a card sticking out of the top that said, "I love you." A nightstand with a pink powder puff in a heart-shaped box. Lacy pillows had fallen from the bed to the floor as if she'd tossed and turned and couldn't get to sleep.

"Jack?"

He threaded his fingers through his still-damp hair and came away with flecks of salt. He needed a shower, a shave and a change into dry clothes. "You never told me why you tracked me down."

"So that gives you the right to sneak in my bedroom window?"

"I don't hear you screaming for help."

She drew her brows together. "What is that supposed to mean?"

"That you want me here."

She sighed. "You were always rash and reckless. When did you become delusional?"

"I thought you were a cop, not a psychiatrist," he countered.

"I'm not a cop anymore." Pain flared in her eyes and then subsided to ashes. "I was fired."

If not for that revealing glimmer of agony in her eyes, he'd have figured she was kidding. But the stark expression on her face told him she'd spoken the truth.

"What happened?"

She shrugged and motioned him toward the window. "Go away, Jack."

"You didn't come to see me about a job, did you?"

"Of course not. Even if I wanted to, which I don't, I'm hardly qualified to work in some paramilitary operation."

"Well, since you didn't track me down to take advantage of my finely cut and totally built body—"

"Not hardly."

"And my ravenous male appetites—"

She snorted.

"You must have wanted me for my brilliant mind and my assessment of your—"

"Careful, Jack."

"—situation?"

His silliness hadn't quite brought out her smile, but it seemed to have decreased her pain to a more tolerable level. She flopped onto her bed with a groan. "I had intended to ask for your help—"

"Which I can't give until you tell me the problem."

"But I changed my mind."

"Okay."

She scowled at him as if by his agreeing with her, he'd disappointed her somehow. Women. If she suspected she could get more from him by remaining secretive, she was too damn smart. He should leave.

He approached the bed. "I said okay."

"I heard you."

"So if you won't talk, I'll just have to torture you until you do."

"Not funny."

"I wasn't going for funny."

"Go away, Jack."

"I'm not leaving." He sat on the bed, crowding her. When she didn't complain about his damp jeans on her sheets, he figured she was testing him. Testing his determination. And he resented the fact that she thought so little of him that she had the need to do so. "What's it going to be? Talk or torture?"

She scooted to the far side of the mattress. "I'll scream if you tickle me."

So she was still ticklish. "You know, Pest—" he resorted to calling her by the old nickname "—I've learned a few strategic moves during my stint in the navy."

"I'll just bet you have. Go away."

"Like how to silence—"

"You wouldn't dare—"

"—a woman with a kiss."

"Oh, for the love of heaven. Don't play your macho BS games with me. I'm impervious to your...charms."

"You're the one playing games. You're the one who tracked me down and—"

"I didn't find what I was looking for."

He ignored the prick of pain at her insult. "You aren't driving me away with your attitude." He stood and paced. Then glanced at her. "Did I pass your test?"

"What are you talking about?"

"You wanted to know if I have staying power, right?"

"Your sexual prowess is of no interest to me."

"You are deliberately misunderstanding."

"Then don't talk in double entendres."

"Look, I still may enjoy sports and my toys—"

"And your women?"

"But you might be interested to know that I work with a team of men, highly skilled and motivated men, who trust me with their lives. So if you can't trust me, the problem is yours—not mine."

She whitened at his words, then lifted her chin and patted the empty spot beside her. "I suppose I deserved that. I'm sorry. It's just that…"

"You hate asking for help? Particularly *my* help. But that's what people do, you know—ask for my help." He sat, still irked that although she'd once hung on his every word and admired his daring, now she seemed to think so little of him.

"Have you ever been fired?" she asked, then answered her own question. "Of course not. That's why you don't understand. In every job I've ever held, I've been commended for my hard work, for putting in the extra effort. I've always been the first one promoted, the first one asked to take on a difficult assignment. In other words I'm accustomed to success. So to be fired, out of the blue, is not just a kick in the teeth, it's made me question my values and everything I believe in.''

''The world isn't fair.''

''You may have always known that.'' She spoke softly. ''I didn't.''

The hurt in her tone was real, so he forgave her her mistrust of him. He might have grown up next door to her, but while her folks were good, steady people, a cop and a teacher, his father was an alcoholic who couldn't keep his job and had taken out his failures on his wife and son. His childhood had made Jack tough, streetwise and determined not to repeat the mistakes of his parents. And now he never drank more than two beers in a night, all too aware of the detrimental effects of alcoholism.

Piper might have been a cop, but she'd always been treated well by her parents, so she still believed that if one played by the rules, one couldn't be hurt.

He understood better than she knew. ''You had great parents who supported your choices. Who protected you.''

''Perhaps they shouldn't have protected me quite so much.'' She curled her legs beneath her, her face miserable. ''Then maybe I could simply accept what happened and move on.''

He took her hand to give her an anchor. ''Tell me.''

''One month before I made detective, I was on traffic duty. I stopped a civilian, a white thirty-year-old male, Vince Edwards, for speeding and ticketed him. Later he came forward and claimed I offered to accept a bribe to let him off the hook.''

Piper? Take a bribe? That was like imagining the sun wouldn't rise in the east. She had more integrity in her pinky than most people had in their entire body.

''But you wrote the ticket?''

She nodded. ''I ticketed the civilian properly, but not only did the ticket disappear from the police station's computer files, someone altered other evidence.''

''What kind of evidence?''

''Every black and white has a GPS. The central computer tracks and logs our movements. According to the computer record, I stopped Vince and let him go within two minutes. It takes about twenty to write a ticket.''

''Surely there are duplicate paper copies?''

''Only one, and it's gone.''

''Didn't you videotape the stop?''

''Yes. But we don't keep the tapes for more than a week. The citizen took a month to come forward.''

''So then what happened?''

''The department investigated and punished me by giving me a ten-day suspension.''

''You said you were fired.''

''I'm getting to that. The incident made the newspaper, and then a second citizen came forward. Leroy James, an African-American man in his mid-fifties, claimed that two years earlier I had openly hinted to him that I would be receptive to a bribe and wouldn't write his ticket in exchange for a hundred dollars. Like I would jeopardize my career and my honor for a hundred bucks?'' She sighed.

''Why did he wait so long to come forward?''

''He claimed he didn't think anyone would believe him, but when he read about the other incident in the paper, he came forward. He took a lie detector test and passed.''

''Lots of people can beat the polygraph machine. They take drugs to calm their nerves.''

''I offered to take the polygraph test, too, but—''

''The department had to follow procedure and do a thorough investigation?''

''You got it. They didn't have enough evidence to press criminal charges against me, but protected the department by firing me.''

''Someone went to a lot of trouble to set you up.''

She squeezed his hand. ''Thanks, Jack.''

He hadn't done anything. ''For what?''

''Believing in me.''

Her sincerity touched him in a way that startled him. He wanted to gather her into his arms to console her. But Jack didn't do the comforting thing well. He kept his relationships light, and although he wasn't the same hell-raiser he'd once been, he stayed away from women like Piper who expected commitment. He certainly didn't get involved in their problems. Or ever think about comforting them.

"What exactly do you want from me?" he asked, his voice rougher than he'd intended.

"I heard that the group you work with—"

"The Shey Group."

"Looks into cases that other people won't take. And that you have computer skills…I'd like to know how someone hacked into the police computer system."

"Maybe they work at the police department."

"I thought of that. But Leslie Green, she's in charge, assures me that none of her people have the codes or the skill to alter the memory without leaving a trace."

"Maybe Leslie—"

"I don't think so. She's an old friend of my mother's. She went out of her way to help me."

"Maybe she's only pretending to be a friend and carries a grudge."

"And maybe your dad will stop drinking tomorrow." Piper dropped his hand and covered the gasp coming out of her mouth. "I'm sorry. That was an awful thing to say. I just meant that people don't change. I didn't mean to…"

Jack took no offense. "Dad is what he is."

"Still, I shouldn't have—"

"It's okay. I no longer believe his behavior reflects on me."

She tilted her head, considering him. "You've grown stronger, more confident, and I've—"

"Gotten a raw deal." He thrummed his fingers on his knee. "Even if I wanted to help, I'm not allowed to take a case on my own without clearing it with my boss.''

''I see. Is this a polite way of telling me that you're unwilling?''

''Let me see what I can do.''

''YOU READY TO DO BUSINESS?''

The instant messaging on the computer screen had the user breaking into a fine sweat. A Google search on the Net hadn't pulled up anything about the mysterious Shey Group. And Jack Donovan's military record was missing. Gone. Either the dude had lied to the cop to impress her, perhaps had even made up the entire story, or someone had carefully erased all information about Jack Donovan.

However, a hacker good enough to break in to the Department of Defense had ways of finding the unfindable. Certain old friends in the military were always open to bribes. In the meantime, there was business to conduct.

The message went back over the Internet with no hint of a problem. ''I was born ready.''

''You take care of the cop?''

Maybe. Maybe not. ''Haven't you heard?''

''Heard what?''

''She was fired.''

''Your doing?''

''Of course.''

''I'm impressed.''

"You're going to be more impressed when you see what I have for you."

"I'm waiting."

"Have you wired the funds to my account?"

"First I need proof that you can deliver."

"Haven't I just done that?"

"I'm not talking about the cop, but about the data I wish to purchase."

PIPER SLEPT SOUNDLY after her late-night conversation with Jack. Her first good night's sleep in weeks. She wanted to believe that her exhaustion had finally taken over. Yet talking to Jack and sharing her problem had been a release of sorts. It seemed that no sooner had she closed her eyes than she was opening them to the morning sun, feeling refreshed and more relaxed than she had in a while—until she spotted Jack Donovan sitting in a chair at the foot of her bed.

She sat up, peered at him and just barely resisted pinching herself to see if she was really awake. Especially when she distinctly recalled him leaving through her window last night. "What are you doing here?"

"Waiting for you to wake up."

"Damn it, Jack. I'm not dressed and you have no—"

"Logan Kincaid said yes. And he's sending me down some specialized equipment."

"Huh?" She rubbed the sleep from her eyes. Why did she always wake up slightly out of sorts? A morning person she was not. And Jack's bright-eyed twinkle only made her grumpier. "Who's Logan Kincaid?"

"My boss. He said we can help you out pro bono."

"I'm not a charity case. I can pay—"

"The Shey Group doesn't take on even a simple mission for less than a million bucks." Jack spoke gently.

A million bucks! No wonder Jack could afford that sexy silver car and the Rolex on his wrist.

Jack had always claimed he'd be a success, and now she believed him, especially if his firm charged those kinds of outrageous prices. But wealth hadn't changed him that much—except for the price of his toys.

He'd gotten his boss to do her a favor, so why was she irritated with him? Probably because she had yet to drink her morning coffee. She didn't function well without a jolt of caffeine.

And while she felt grubby, he'd shaved, showered and donned jeans and a shirt. Plus, he used her window like a revolving door, coming and going as if he had every right to enter her bedroom whenever he pleased.

However annoyed she might be, she couldn't overlook the fact that he'd gone out of his way to help her. And during his vacation, too.

"Thanks, Jack. Please thank your boss for me."

"No problem." His gaze dropped to her legs. "You might want to dress so I'm not so distracted—then we need to talk some more."

He couldn't see any more leg than if she'd been wearing shorts. However, just knowing that she could distract him had her humming, and she took her time striding into the bathroom. She might not be experienced with men, but she did know how to use the assets she'd been born with.

Jack climbed back out the window. "I'll pick you up in ten minutes."

"Twenty." Piper didn't flirt—hardly ever—yet she couldn't resist teasing Jack. "And I'll give you another kiss if you bring me a cup of strong black coffee."

She thought he grunted, and she grinned, pleased with herself. Twenty minutes later, dressed in a tank top, capri pants and sandals, she met Jack in her driveway. Knowing he'd want to ride with the top down, she'd tied her hair into a ponytail and wore dark sunglasses.

When he handed her a mug filled to the brim with coffee, she grinned and leaned over to kiss him. "Thanks."

He tried to give her his cheek, but with a wider grin she reached for his jaw, turned his head and kissed his mouth, leaving a smudge of lipstick. With her thumb she wiped away the smudge.

"When did you turn into such a flirt?" he muttered, but there was no heat in his complaint.

"Can't a girl be happy an old friend's come back home and is willing to help her out of a jam?"

He pulled out of her drive. "We were never friends,

and if you spill that coffee on my new leather seats, I will resort to torture.''

''Of course we were friends.''

''Oh, really?'' He drove with the same abandon that she remembered, yet still managed to adhere to the speed limit. ''I remember this flat-chested pesky kid with braces who took great pleasure in interrupting my dates.''

Piper might have developed late, but now she arched her back—in case he hadn't noticed—showing off a curvy 36C bustline. ''Watching you was much more informative than my sex-ed class. You were my best source of information,'' she teased. ''If not for you, I might have made it to the high school prom before I knew that kids could make love in the back seat of a car.''

He swore under his breath. ''You watched?''

She chuckled. ''Only until you took off her shirt. When you ducked down onto the seat—''

''And you could no longer see?''

''I got bored.''

''Thank God.'' He let out an exaggerated sigh.

She patted his thigh, noting the hard muscles beneath her fingers. ''But we *were* friends. I seem to recall how you warned off a certain seventh-grade boy from peeking at me through a hole in the wall in the girls' locker room.''

He raised an eyebrow. ''You knew about that?''

''And how you fixed my fort after the roof collapsed.''

"Mmm. Course, I had ulterior motives. I used to bring my dates there."

"And when I was six you saved me from drowning at the beach."

"I'm just a knight in shining armor."

"Rusty armor." She sipped her coffee. "Where are we going?"

"To speak to the civilians you allegedly bribed."

"Why?"

"I want to look them in the eye, check out where they live and who they live with. And I want to gauge how they react when they see you show up on their doorstep."

"I have files on both of them."

"I'll read them later. I want my first impressions to be my own."

"Okay." She gave him Vince Edwards's address, which she knew from memory. Many times since her accusers had come forward she'd wanted to drive to their homes to confront them with their lies. But her union rep and her attorney had advised her against it. Listening to them had gotten her fired. And her research had never found a reason for the men to lie about her. She'd never found a motive. Or one shred of evidence that the two men had ever known one another. With nothing else to lose, she was willing to follow Jack's lead.

He pulled up in front of an apartment complex. According to her file, Vince Edwards worked as a mechanic for a delivery company and earned about forty thousand a year. He'd never been in trouble with the law and had been married and divorced twice. Piper hoped he didn't work on Sundays.

After climbing two flights of stairs to the third floor, Jack knocked on the door. A white-haired woman answered the door, her eyes red rimmed with tears. "Yes?"

"We're looking for Vince, ma'am."

"Are you a friend of his?"

"This is business."

"I hope he doesn't owe you money."

"No, ma'am."

"That's good, because my son died last night in a car crash."

Chapter Three

One loose thread gone. One more to tie off.

The work had to be done with the same care as carrying out a secret military operation. Piper Payne might have been fired, but as an ex-cop, whose mother was also an ex-cop, she still had connections. Killing her could have serious repercussions, repercussions that could bring law enforcement to the door. So for now, she could live and take the heat for her "crime."

The primary concern was the man. Jack Donovan might be a real problem. After an exhaustive and fruitless search on the Net, a bribe to an old friend in Special Forces had finally produced the needed information. The Shey Group was a private, for-hire team of ex-military heroes. And Jack Donovan was their pilot.

With him in the picture, extra precautions had to be taken. And if necessary, as a very last resort, the daring duo could be taken out.

But first there were other less drastic actions to be tried.

VINCE HAD DIED *just last night?* A coincidence or bad luck? Piper wondered. During her years as a street cop and then these past six months as a detective she'd learned to trust her instincts, and right now those instincts were screaming that Vince's death was no accident. If his death proved to be murder, setting her up probably hadn't been his idea. However, a good cop never jumped to conclusions.

"Mrs. Edwards, I hate to intrude on your sorrow, but could we come in and speak to you for a few minutes?" Jack asked. "My name is Jack Donovan. I had wanted to ask your son about an investigation I'm working on. I wonder if I could ask you instead?"

The grief-stricken woman opened the door and gestured for them to enter the apartment, which was overcrowded with furniture. A sagging couch, a torn love seat and two tattered recliners left little room to walk. Dozens of pictures were thumbtacked to the wall, mostly of half-naked women. Newspapers and magazines sat in lopsided stacks against one wall and lay scattered across a scratched coffee table. A black cat curled up on one arm of the sofa, seemingly undisturbed by their presence.

"Would you care for a cola or coffee?" Mrs. Edwards asked politely.

"No, thanks."

Mrs. Edwards sat down, motioning toward the recliners across from her. Jack took a seat, while Piper remained standing beside him. She had a hundred questions in her head. Her innate curiosity had made her a good cop and had enabled her to pull her share of criminals off the street. She'd even wondered if one of those criminals might have gotten even with her by setting up the faked bribery charges, but she'd never found a connection between anyone she'd put behind bars and either of the men who'd accused her of taking bribes. Her investigation had gone nowhere but down dead ends, so she wanted to see how Jack would steer the conversation.

Jack looked around the room. "Did your son have a computer?"

"Doesn't everyone?"

"What did he use it for?"

"He liked to play games. That was why wife number one divorced him."

"Was he into hacking?"

"He barely graduated high school."

The facts that Vince had worked a blue-collar job and hadn't done well in school didn't mean he wasn't some kind of self-taught computer guru—but the odds of that were unlikely.

"Was your son in any kind of trouble?" he asked, his voice sympathetic.

Mrs. Edwards frowned. "What do you mean?"

"Did he have any problems at work?"

She shook her head. "He's been at the same company for the last five years."

"Was he into drugs or alcohol? Gambling, maybe?"

Vince's mother might have been distressed, but she

was one sharp lady. "Are you saying Vince's car wreck might not have been an accident? The police didn't say that, but they didn't give me any details."

"What do you think?" Jack asked.

Up until this point, Mrs. Edwards had struck Piper as honest and forthright. A mother in mourning, dealing with shock and grief and anger at her sudden loss. Yet, at Jack's question, she hesitated a moment too long, as if considering her next words with care—too much care.

Mrs. Edwards wrung her hands. "Just why are you people here?"

Jack ignored her question and asked one of his own, an interrogation technique that Piper had often employed successfully as a detective. "Did Vince have a girlfriend?"

"Some tart named Ellen Jo Dasher. She still has some clothes in Vince's closet."

"How long had they been together?" Jack asked.

She shrugged.

"Does he still have contact with his ex-wives?"

"I don't keep track of Vince's love life. We aren't…weren't that close."

"What about his male friends?"

"The guys at work, but no one in particular that he was especially close to."

The picture she'd drawn of her son was that of a loner, possibly someone emotionally dysfunctional— but not necessarily a criminal. Piper still couldn't think of any motive for the man to have set her up.

"Did your son come into any unexpected money recently?"

"What do you mean?"

"Did he say he'd won big at lotto? Or bingo?"

"Vince was always broke. He usually called when he needed money—which he never paid back."

"How much money?"

"Whatever he could weasel out of me. Fifty here, a hundred there. I live on my telephone company pension, and I'm not a rich woman."

Jack stood and handed Mrs. Edwards a business card. "I'm very sorry for your loss. If you come across any information that might mean someone was after your son, or you just want to talk, please feel free to contact me."

Piper had remained silent long enough. "Ma'am, my name is Piper Payne. I used to be *Detective* Piper Payne." Piper watched the woman's eyes for any sign of recognition, but saw none.

"You used to be?"

"Your son never mentioned me?"

Mrs. Edwards lifted a pair of glasses from her neck to the bridge of her nose and peered at Piper. "You don't look like his type. Are you one of his ex—"

"Your son accused me of taking a bribe."

"Excuse me?"

"To get him out of a traffic ticket."

For the first time, Mrs. Edwards avoided their gazes. "I don't know anything about that."

"I was fired. And I was hoping you might know why he would lie."

"My son wasn't a liar. At least, he never lied to me." Mrs. Edwards sighed. "You might want to speak to Ellen—maybe she knows more...." She wrote Ellen's address on a piece of paper and handed it to Piper. "Good luck, dear."

Despite Mrs. Edwards's seeming cooperation, Piper couldn't help wondering what the woman was hiding. As they walked back to Jack's car, she wished she had more to go on than a hunch.

"She wasn't telling us the whole truth," Jack said, confirming her own suspicions.

"Why did she feel she needed to cover for a son who is no longer alive?"

"Maybe habit." Jack opened her car door for her. "And lots of people don't want to speak badly of the dead."

"I wish we had copies of his credit card bills, bank statements and phone records."

"That can be arranged." Jack grinned at her, that wide, reckless grin that made her believe he was up to something rash.

"I don't want you breaking the law."

"Why? You going to arrest me?"

"Jack—"

"I won't do anything my boss doesn't approve of."

She sighed. "Why doesn't that make me feel better?"

"Look, you played by the rules and got fired.

Who's going to complain if we bend them a little? Certainly not Vince Edwards. He's dead.''

"Is that how you salve your conscience?"

"Nope. That's how I salve yours."

"Jack—"

"Let me do what I do best." He donned his sunglasses. "Now, what kind of info can you get from the police department?"

"What do you need?"

"Anything you can find out about Vince Edwards's car accident."

He'd changed the subject to distract her, but she really didn't want to argue, especially when he was trying to help her. "I still have a few friends in the department. If I can't get my hands on that accident report, I can probably find out what's in it."

Jack handed her the cell phone. "Make the call."

While Jack started the car and drove, she spoke to the police officer in charge of writing up Vince's accident.

Dissatisfied with the answers she'd received, she flipped the phone closed and handed it back to Jack. "They'll have more for me after the mechanics go over the car. It appears to have been a two-car accident on a mostly deserted road. The other driver left the scene, but initial findings indicate that the paint scratches came from a dark-green car. They are hoping to match the factory paint to a make or model."

"Any witnesses?"

"None. When Vince's car collided with a telephone

pole, he died instantly.'' She glanced at Jack. ''It could be murder. Or a simple hit-and-run by a drunk driver or just someone afraid to come forward.''

''Even if Vince was murdered, his death might not have anything to do with you,'' Jack reminded her.

''So are we going to Vince's girlfriend's house next?''

''First I'd rather visit the other man who accused you—before he also has an accident.''

LEROY JAMES LIVED in a stuccoed two-story colonial house in an upscale neighborhood on the intracoastal waterway. The house boasted a broad front porch and tall white columns that were welcoming yet pretentious. The deed-restricted community was the kind with lots of rules. No garage door could face the street. No satellite dishes could be mounted on the roofs and no unsightly motor homes or pickup trucks could park in the driveways. The landscaping was lush, the underground sprinkler systems kept the grass green and the palm trees healthy, even in the tropical heat of summer.

Jack parked on the street. ''Nice place.''

''Real estate like this costs three, four hundred grand, easy.'' Piper frowned. ''I can't imagine anyone who lives here accusing me just to make a few bucks.''

Jack didn't turn off the engine, allowing the AC to keep running. ''Why do you think someone might have paid these men to lie about you?''

"Because they are strangers to me. And I can't find anything Vince and Leroy have in common. They didn't attend the same schools or hang out with the same crowds. And neither one of them seems to have connections to anyone I put away."

"What's Leroy do to earn the big bucks?"

The lot was large enough to see between the homes to the waterway. Motorboats traveled up and down behind the house. If she had a house like this, she'd be sunning by the pool or out on her yacht. "He got his money the old-fashioned way—he married it."

"He doesn't work?"

"He's a songwriter, but he's never made a dime."

"What's his wife do?"

"Runs an investment firm. Her father was a big-time football star. The family has lots of connections."

Jack took about two seconds to put things together. "They leaned on the police chief to get you fired?"

"If they did, they didn't have to lean hard. A cop's word is her bond."

"What do you mean?"

"Once a police officer is caught lying or taking a bribe, he or she can no longer work effectively in the court system."

"Why not?"

"If the chief had let me keep my job and I went to court to testify, every time I took the stand the defense attorney would ask if I'd ever been caught lying or taking a bribe. Since I would have to answer 'Yes,' juries wouldn't believe whatever testimony I gave.

The theory is that if I lied once, I'd lie again, and there would be no convictions so long as I was involved in the case.''

"Okay. I get it." Jack turned off the car and pressed a button. The hardtop slid out of the trunk and snapped into place. "You've never spoken to Leroy, right?"

"Correct."

"So how do you know so much about him?"

She supposed there was no harm in admitting her indiscretion to Jack. "There was an official police investigation. A friend let me read the file."

He glanced at her, his lips close to a smirk. "Isn't that against the rules?"

"Shut up, Jack."

She slammed the door and took pleasure in his wince at her harsh treatment of his fine automobile. She didn't know if she was more annoyed that he found it amusing she was so uncomfortable breaking a rule or that she'd actually broken it. It was almost as if he expected her to be perfect. Well, she was far from perfect.

A disgrace to the force, she'd been fired for lack of moral character, for cheating and lying and taking a bribe. And most of her former colleagues could barely look her in the eyes. She avoided the department, and since her entire life had revolved around her work, she'd lost not only her job, but her social life, her support group and her friends.

Jack rang the doorbell, but no one answered.

"Now what?" she asked.

"We check with the neighbors." He gestured to the houses next door. "Why don't I go right, you go left. We'll meet back at my car and compare notes."

She raised an eyebrow. "You trust me to ask the right questions?"

He grinned. "As far as I'm concerned, there are no bad questions, just bad women."

"And the badder they are, the better you like them?" Some things never changed. Was he trying to tell her he wasn't interested in her? She already knew that. She was too much of a Goody Two-shoes for Jack. But that didn't mean she couldn't fantasize about what being with him would be like.

She'd never heard any complaints from the girls he'd gone through like a mower through a hayfield. Not even when he dumped them. But then, he tended to pick girls who didn't expect much except a good time.

Apparently Jack hadn't changed. But she had. She didn't want to hold out for Mr. Right anymore—suppose he never came along? She'd played by the rules all her life and all she'd ended up with was disappointment and pain. Piper needed a dose of Jack's outlook—fun for fun's sake. Pleasure while it lasted. Flushed at the peculiar direction her thoughts had taken, she shoved the idea to the back of her mind—to be reexamined for flaws late that night when she couldn't sleep due to wanting a man she couldn't have.

Ten minutes later they were back in the car. She was grateful for the car's magnificent air-conditioning, and she appreciated that Jack had changed the convertible back into a hardtop before she got a second-degree burn from the leather seat. "You tell me what you learned first."

Jack shifted the car into forward gear and spoke while he drove. "The family consists of Leroy, his wife, Jenette, and two teenage daughters. They're away on vacation. Went to Amelia Island, a classy resort near Jacksonville. He spends a lot of time on the computer. They have a high-speed connection." Jack turned into traffic. "What did you get?"

"Apparently the couple fights a lot."

"Money problems?"

She shook her head. "According to the neighbor, who seems to be a busybody of the highest order, he's been cheating on her with some woman he met online in a chat room. Apparently he told the neighbor's husband, who told her. His wife doesn't know where he's spending his time or with whom, but she's complaining that he's never home. I tried to get the name of the mistress, but the neighbor didn't know it."

Jack patted her thigh. "You did well. That will give me a lot to go on."

"How?"

"Once I get his credit card statement, I'll look for hotel bills and repeated phone calls. From there I might get the mistress's number and soon after her address."

"So what?"

"I bet she'll tell us more than the wife. Especially

since the man is trying to appease his wife with a family vacation. The mistress will be miffed. You know what they say about a woman scorned…."

She twisted in her seat to observe Jack. "You do more for the Shey Group than pilot the team, don't you?"

He evaded her question without changing his expression. "What makes you ask?"

"You're too well acquainted with hacking your way into private—"

"I can hold my own. Most ex-SEALs can, and I trained in—well, it's still classified. But another team member has even more expertise than me. If I run into trouble, I may have to ask Ryker for help. He'll know how to hack the police system—"

"He can do that?"

"I can do that—but I might get caught. Ryker knows how to go in and out without leaving a trail."

"I don't want—"

"You want your job back or not?"

"But your methods…"

"Work."

JACK AND PIPER HAD no luck finding Vince's girl-friend, Ellen Jo Dasher, who lived in a run-down duplex. Her neighbors didn't answer their doors, so Jack and Piper ate a late lunch, then he dropped her off at her home and arrived back at his parents' house just in time to sign for the equipment Logan had sent him via special military transport.

Jack's father staggered out onto the porch. "What's that?" Bleary-eyed from the bottle of cheap vodka he'd been swilling, he glared at the crates before Jack could lug them out of sight into the garage.

"Electronic gear."

"You steal it?"

"Nope. It's all legit."

His mother joined his father on the porch, her face tight with disapproval. "You spent your good money on that junk?"

His mother had no idea that his gear was necessary to his mission, and Jack had no intention of explaining anything to her. He'd learned a long time ago that they would never approve of him, his career or his success. Coming home had been a mistake.

"You aren't bringing that rubbish into my house."

"Why not?"

"Because…because…because it might explode," she finished, quite proud of herself for thinking up her answer.

"Computers don't explode, Mom."

"Computers are unnatural."

"Right, because if God wanted people to have computers, he would have given us an Intel chip for a brain." Jack couldn't check his sarcasm. He knew his mom was frustrated that she'd had only one child, a boy, who refused to help her care for her "sick" husband. Years ago Jack had tried to get his father to Alcoholics Anonymous. But his father liked being an alcoholic and his mother liked being an enabler—so she could claim to whoever would listen that she was a saint to put up with him.

His father peered at him in confusion, probably because he was seeing double. "Are you making fun of your mother?"

His mom didn't wait for Jack to answer. She pointed to his gear. "You are not bringing that stuff into my home."

Jack would have loaded up his car, but the sleek two-seater couldn't possibly hold all his equipment. "I'll see if the Paynes will store it for me."

He hadn't wanted to bring Piper into this part of his operation, but he preferred to avoid a hotel where many people had a room key. This equipment was expensive, specialized and not altogether legal for civilian use. His boss had close ties to the military, and the team often worked with top secret equipment but had been warned not to flaunt it.

So Jack made three trips, lugging the crates over to the Payne house while his folks sat on their porch and glared at him. He'd hoped that the ten-year separation would have caused them to mellow, maybe miss their only son. Instead they seemed just as determined to drive him off now as they had when he was a kid.

Which was one of the reasons Jack never envisioned his own marriage or becoming a father. His folks had set such a poor example. He had no idea how to raise a kid the right way. But he did know better than to try.

When he rang the doorbell, he expected Piper's parents to answer. But Piper opened the door and took one look at his armload before reaching for the top crate. "Let me help."

"My folks..."

"It's okay." She grinned at him. "This way I can keep an eye on...your equipment."

Was she deliberately flirting with him? Most likely the double entendre had been accidental. "I intended to keep you informed."

"But now we can work together." Her tone was light and happy.

She had no more idea how this equipment worked than his parents, yet she invited him inside without hesitation. She always had. Her home had been a refuge when things got bad at his house, her parents welcoming. And if Piper suspected that his gear might not be exactly street legal, she didn't indicate it by her expression or attitude.

"There's an extra bedroom on the second floor that my mom was fitting out for a real estate office."

He followed her up the stairs, noting that she had really nice buns to go with her long legs. In fact, if he hadn't known Piper and had met her at a bar, he would have hit on her immediately. For the umpteenth time that day he reminded himself she wasn't that kind of girl. She was the fall-in-love, get-married-and-have-a-bundle-of-kids kind of woman.

"Your mom's a real estate broker?"

"A saleswoman—or she will be if she ever passes the state exam. Math isn't her strong suit."

"I thought she was retired."

"She's not ready. Dad's not ready, either. But he has more hobbies to keep him going. He loves to golf and fish. That's where he is right now—out hooking snapper."

They made several more trips, and he appreciated the fact that Piper didn't seem all that interested in his equipment—at least, his electronic equipment. He'd caught her staring at his buttocks when he ascended the stairs ahead of her, and when they locked gazes she blushed—but she didn't drop her eyes.

He'd been the first to look away. Great. Next she'd have him tongue-tied, a state he hadn't been in since ninth grade when a senior had shown him what making love was all about.

"What are you thinking?" she asked.

"About you," he teased. And then he let his tone turn serious. "I was wondering if you were up for a little breaking and entering?"

BREAKING AND ENTERING?

The lovey-dovey duo should go find a room. But no, they couldn't leave the investigation alone. Clearly they weren't going to give up. And if they got to the source and applied the right pressure, Leroy might cave.

Leroy was a weak link. But then, he was a weak man, ruled by his dick. Caught between his voluptuous mistress and his rich wife, he'd set himself up to be taken advantage of. So he deserved what he got.

And Donovan and Payne thought he was on vacation. Wrong. But a clever person could use that mistake to advantage.

Their incorrect information could be the means to do them in. Especially if they planned an illegal break-in.

A fist of fury slammed the keyboard. If the cop and her almost-lover kept asking questions, eventually business would suffer. And with the biggest deal of the century about to set up a lifetime of luxury retirement, now was not the time to allow such peons to persevere.

Strength, determination and cunning would win the day.

But the Shey Group angle could prove troublesome. Dealing with even the one team member was irksome. An accident would have to be set up with care. With no strings leading back to the source. Because if the team descended like a horde of swarming hornets, the sting could be painful and severe.

Careful planning was in order. Planning that would end their interference—for good.

Chapter Four

"You want us to break in to a building?" Piper tried and failed to keep her voice from rising at her sharp disappointment in Jack. Did he really have so little regard for the law? Jack had done some crazy things in his life, but no matter the end, she couldn't justify his means. She'd sworn to uphold the law and was working to clear her name. How could she go along with him and be such a hypocrite? "Breaking and entering is illegal."

"No need to worry. We won't get caught." He grinned that charming grin at her, the one that used to make his old girlfriends practically swoon. Jack had always had the ability to talk both males and females into his reckless schemes, and somehow he always came out smelling cleaner than breath mint.

And he was deliberately missing her point. She didn't bother keeping the exasperation from her tone. "Do you really think that the possibility of getting caught is all that I object to?"

"Look, I'm hoping to acquire information on who might have framed you."

She set down the last crate and turned to face him. "That sounds good, Jack. But what about the illegal part?"

"We already covered that." He used a screwdriver to open the first crate, his hands swift and strong. He'd always been handy, fixing his motorcycle and later his car. One summer he'd even worked as a sports car mechanic. He could probably assemble a computer with his eyes shut.

"Breaking and entering is wrong, Jack."

"Yeah." He pulled out a sleek computer with a wide, flat monitor, handling the equipment with the tenderness a father might give to a baby. He ran wires to a plug and hooked into her mother's Internet service provider. There was no fumbling, no reading directions, no hesitation—obviously he'd put this equipment together many times before.

"We have privacy laws to protect the innocent."

"Yeah, but I'm not interested in the innocent, only the guilty."

"Before you hack in, you have no way of knowing if you are investigating the innocent or the guilty."

"Yeah."

Her fingers itched to slap the oh-so-charming grin right off his oh-so-handsome face. He was toying with her values and her sense of right and wrong, and she didn't appreciate him challenging her principles, not one little bit. But when he agreed with her, she had no idea how to argue with him.

"Exactly *where* do you want to break in?"

"Leroy's house. The man lied about you. He broke the law first. And as a former police officer, you should be committed to justice, even for yourself. He's on vacation, so it shouldn't be too difficult."

"Why do you need to go inside?"

"It's easier to break in to his computer if I'm there in person." He turned on his computer, and while the systems loaded, he pulled her over to the window seat. "You don't have to come with me, but I could use a lookout."

"Can't you hack into his system from here?"

"Maybe. But it's more difficult and I would probably leave a trail that might lead back to us. You needn't come inside. Just be my eyes and ears."

"That house probably has an alarm."

"I'll take care of it."

"How?"

"I have a device that will override his system."

"What about the lock?"

"Not a problem." He took her hand and rubbed her fingers. "We won't steal or damage anything. If he's innocent, no harm will be done. He'll never even know we've been there."

Maddeningly, he could be the most persuasive man. He made his plan sound so reasonable and made her sound irrational for not going along.

Jack squeezed her hand. "And if he's guilty—"

"The evidence you get won't be legal, since we obtained it illegally."

"We aren't going to prove your case in a court of law."

"But—"

"We want the charges from the two citizens dismissed. And we can do that if we have enough evidence. You're going to have to trust me." Jack released her hand and returned to the computer. "Give me a sec. I need to run Ryker's *Search and Compile* program."

If he'd just changed the subject to distract her, he'd only partially succeeded. Yet she wouldn't forget her misgivings—misgivings that went deep and straight to her core. She'd become a police officer to serve the community, to protect people, to get criminals off the streets. And for the most part, the system worked.

"What's *Search and Compile?*"

"The program looks for aberrations in a pattern."

She followed him to the computer and peered over his shoulder. He typed in the names "Vince Edwards" and "Leroy James," his fingers dancing over the keys in a blur. Then he hit the "enter" key and laced his hands behind his head, a satisfied gleam in his eyes.

"Ryker wrote a program that will automatically search for information about these people," he explained. "It will call up phone bills, credit card bills, driving records, arrest records, real estate owned, schools attended, IRS records—"

"I get the idea."

"The data will be placed and stored in convenient files. Then the computer goes to work pulling out things that don't fit a pattern."

"You just lost me."

"Suppose that every August Leroy takes his family to Disneyland, but this year he goes to the beach. The computer will kick that fact out. Or suppose his average credit card purchase is twenty dollars, and he suddenly buys a two-thousand-dollar diamond ring, the computer will kick that out for me to peruse."

"Clever."

"Ryker Stevens is a genius and his program is very thorough. It's also slow. And might take days to find anything significant. But eventually, if there is a connection between Vince and Leroy, the computer will find it."

During her investigation she'd done background searches of both men, but she had only skimmed the surface before she'd been pulled off the case. The computer could turn up many things that she hadn't had a chance to research. "Like maybe they went to Cub Scouts together?"

"Or have a friend in common—one that maybe you put away in the slammer."

She'd thought of that possibility and had gone through her records. If there was a connection between the two men who'd accused her of taking a bribe, she'd never found one. "So we wait."

"And while we wait, we dig around at Leroy's house."

Talk about a one-track mind. She used to call Jack persistent. But the truth was closer to stubborn. Damn stubborn.

"Dig around? I thought you wanted to see what's on his computer?"

"That, too. While I'm busy cracking his password, you can check the house trash cans and his coat pockets, his drawers, his—"

"I thought I didn't have to go inside?"

"You don't, but if I have to do everything, it'll take longer."

And increase their chances of getting caught. She suspected he'd known all along that she would give in. No way could she let him take that kind of risk for her while she played it safe. "I know how to do a search."

"Good." He winked at her. "Then you can be useful. I do so adore a useful woman."

She rolled her eyes heavenward. "I didn't say I was going with you."

"Yeah, but if I leave you alone, you're going to miss me."

"Aren't you ever serious?"

"You mean you wouldn't miss me?" He clapped one hand over his heart. "I'm hurt."

"Jack?"

"Yeah?"

"I don't want to do this." Her protest was more for form. She didn't want to appear to give in too easily.

"That's cool. I'll go alone."

Just like that, he was letting her off the hook. But how could she stay safe at home and let him risk a felony—when he was doing this for her?

"I can't let you do that."

"You can't stop me."

She shook her head. "That's not what I meant. I can't let you go alone."

His eyes narrowed. "But you just said—"

"I don't want to do this—but I will."

"You sure?"

"Yes."

He grinned. "Good. It's going to be a blast."

PIPER'S STOMACH CLENCHED in fear, as it did when she pulled over a citizen during a traffic stop. A police officer never knew if the person behind the wheel or a passenger might pull a gun, or step on the gas and flee. She had to keep herself ready and alert and wary, on edge enough to react quickly if necessary.

And breaking in to Leroy's house in the dark gave her the same jolt of adrenaline. Chances were they'd get in and out without a hitch. But the possibilities of being caught were endless. The family could come home early. A neighbor could spot them and call 911. An attack dog could charge out of the den.

Piper wrapped her fear under tight control. As promised, Jack had gotten them inside without a problem.

He had used a remote control device to open the automatic garage door and driven right inside as if they had every right to be there. Hopefully no neighbors were up at 3:00 a.m. to notice them.

Jack was busy at the door that led from the garage to the home's interior. She shone a penlight so he could attach some device to the alarm system's wiring. Within ten seconds he had the red blinking light turning to green, and she released a pent-up breath.

"You'll be fine," Jack whispered.

"If we don't get caught."

"That's what makes this so much fun."

She followed him into the kitchen. "Yeah, right."

"It's like having sex that very first time. You don't know what to expect and that adds to the thrill."

"I wouldn't know."

"Your first time wasn't exciting?" Jack led her through the kitchen and into the den. He shone his light on the computer keyboard, then checked the windows to make sure the screen wouldn't reflect outside.

Piper didn't want to discuss her nonexistent sex life, which was no one's business but hers. Anxious to get their search over with as quickly as possible, she headed toward the staircase. "I'll start in the master bedroom upstairs and work my way down."

"Be careful not to let your light hit any mirrors," Jack reminded her. He'd already turned on the computer, and the hum seemed loud in the quiet house.

"How long are we going to be here?" she asked.

"It's just like sex. We take as long as we need."

"I wouldn't know," she muttered, again.

She reached the fifth or sixth step before Jack spoke again. "Piper, don't tell me that you're still a virgin?"

"I've never broken the law before." She deliberately avoided his question. She didn't want to admit that she'd once dreamed of losing her virginity to him. Nor did she want to admit that she still found him hard to resist.

Before he could say anything else, she left him behind. While she wasn't ashamed of her virginal status, she wasn't sure she wanted Jack to know about it. She didn't want him to think she hadn't had several opportunities. She had. But somehow she always ended things before she got that far.

The thin elastic gloves Jack had insisted she wear were the same issue detectives used to avoid contaminating a crime scene. So she had no trouble opening drawers, rifling through jacket pockets in her search through Leroy's things. Either his wife was a meticulous housekeeper or he was a neat freak.

She didn't find so much as a slip of paper in the suits and pants hanging in his walk-in closet or in the polo shirts and boxers folded neatly in his drawers. The laundry basket was empty, as were the trash cans—almost as if the house had been sanitized by an expert.

Not so much as a dirty sock under the bed. She checked the medicine cabinet in the bathroom. Nothing. When she opened the nightstand's drawer, she found a pink address book, probably the wife's. She flipped through it, surprised at the number of entries.

Everything from baby-sitters to doctors to the local veterinarian.

Leroy's side held a Bible, a half pack of breath mints, two condoms and a pair of reading glasses.

She hoped Jack was having better luck. She didn't bother with the children's rooms and headed back downstairs. Maybe they had a home office—although that was unlikely, since the family computer was in the den.

"Find anything?" she asked Jack.

"Leroy spent the majority of his online time in chat rooms."

"What kind of chat rooms?"

"He was cruising for women. Young women. His latest love interest went by the name of Baby Cakes." Jack typed and spoke to her at the same time. "I've inserted a worm into his machine. I think it might give me Baby Cakes's ISP address."

"Baby Cakes?" Had she seen that name in the wife's address book? She'd thought it was a store for baby clothing or birthday cakes. Hadn't paid it any attention.

She hurried back upstairs, pulled out the address book and there it was. Keeping the address book, she hurried back down the stairs. "Jack, I think I have Baby Cakes's phone number."

"You found Leroy's address book?"

"This book is pink. I think it's his wife's address book. Look." She turned to the *B*s and pointed.

Jack wrote down the phone number on a pad next to the computer. "You think they're into swinging?"

"A threesome?" She shook her head. "It's more likely the wife knew about his cheating and was keeping track."

"What for?"

"So he couldn't hit her for a big divorce settlement?" she guessed. "I wonder if there are other women and she knew about them. If only we could copy this book."

"Just keep it."

"That's stealing."

"Borrowing. If it makes you feel better, we'll mail it back when we're done—anonymously, of course." Jack went to an Internet site and typed in Baby Cakes's phone number. "We now have an address." He wrote it down on the pad.

"Are you about done?"

"Yeah. I've altered the .exe file on this computer."

"Which means?"

"That I can now get into his system from your house."

"We can leave?"

He powered down the machine. "Yes."

"Jack."

He reached over to unplug his electronic device. "Just a sec."

"Jack."

"What?"

"There's a car coming down the street."

"So?"

"It doesn't have any lights on."

"Almost done."

"Hurry."

"Why?"

"Because the car is now turning into Leroy's driveway."

"Shut off your penlight. Get behind the desk."

She expected him to say he would handle the intruder. Instead, he hunkered down beside her. "Shouldn't we go out the back door?"

"Shh."

"We should go while we can."

"Shh."

She lowered her voice, her body pressed close to his, her lips next to his ear. "What the hell are we doing here?"

"Seeing who shows up."

JACK DIDN'T BELIEVE that a thief had just happened to pick Leroy's house while they were inside. And he'd bet his Mercedes that Leroy hadn't come home early with his family at four in the morning.

When a key scraped in the lock of the front door, Jack tensed. He heard a steady beeping sound, a footstep in the tiled hallway, then nothing but more incessant beeping. No doubt the intruder had stopped to turn off the alarm and was puzzled, since it was already off. But what the hell was that beeping? It sounded like...

"Get your clothes off," he whispered. "Now."

Jack pulled his shirt over his head, kicked off his

shoes and was peeling off his pants before Piper began to move.

"What?"

He put a finger to her mouth. Shook his head. And prayed she'd follow his lead. He whispered, "Come on, Pest. I'll show you mine if you show me yours."

They didn't have much time. Jack peeled off his briefs, rolled his clothes into a ball and tossed them as far as he could into the living room. He pushed his shoes in the opposite direction. Now he was totally naked, except for his gun in one hand and his car keys and his pad filled with notes in the other.

Beside him Piper had taken off her shirt and slacks. She was fumbling over her bra.

"Make me a happy man, woman," he whispered, then placed the pad and keys down to unsnap her bra hooks. "Get them off fast."

Bless her. She followed his lead and peeled down to nothing, balled up her clothes and tossed them.

He scooped up his keys and notes. Smelled gasoline. Whoever was in the house knew they were there. And they weren't coming to get them. They were setting a fire to burn them alive.

They had to get out. Fast.

Hopefully the arsonist was working alone and no one was waiting outside.

Grabbing Piper's hand, he squeezed hard, then bolted toward the garage, tugging her with him. They leaped into the car.

"Get your seat belt on, now." Jack started the engine, revved it. Rammed the car into Reverse. Crashed through the fiberglass door.

Beside him, Piper screamed. "Are you insane?"

Jack concentrated on driving. He jammed on his brakes and burned rubber as he spun the car into a controlled one-eighty. He shifted into Forward and squealed out of the neighborhood. Behind him flames were already leaping out of the downstairs windows and doors. And he had caught sight of a silhouette darting away through the bushes.

He glanced at Piper. "You okay?" She wasn't covering her breasts with her arms. Even when he turned his head and looked, she didn't flinch from his gaze. Although it was dark, he got more than an eyeful. Piper was built. And half of him felt as though he were peeping at his kid sister. The other half felt on fire. He forced his eyes back on the road.

"Tell me you had a reason for making me get naked."

He had no problem teasing her. "You mean other than wanting to see your big, beautiful—"

"Jack, don't start. I'm not feeling particularly heroic running around bare-assed, and you'd better start explaining before I—"

"Before you what?"

"Come unglued."

She didn't sound as if she was losing it. In fact, she sounded sexy as hell, but perhaps the huskiness in her tone was because she didn't drive naked in a getaway car every day. Or perhaps she was as stimulated by the adventure as he was. Either way, he had no intention of indulging himself with Piper—even if she looked like his perfect fantasy.

Think about the case—not her breasts, damn it.

"It's odd that someone showed up at the house so soon after we got there."

"Were we tailed?"

"I would have picked up on a tail. But remember that beeping?"

"Yes."

"It came from a tracking device. Someone planted a bug on us. I'm hoping the bug isn't in my car. But probably it was on you."

"So that's why we ditched our clothes."

"Was your wallet in your fanny pack?"

"Yes, but I left my identification at home, so we don't have to worry that arson investigators will know we were there."

"Good."

She shifted in her seat. Her flesh must be sticking to the leather. She couldn't possibly be trying to draw his attention, could she? If she had been anyone else but Piper, he would have thought she might be receptive to a little... Naw. He was letting the nudity situation override his common sense. And while he was thinking thoughts he shouldn't be, she pulled together the facts. "You said all those double entendres so it would sound as if we were about to make love because someone might have been listening?"

"Yeah."

"Suppose I had taken you up on your offer?"

He ignored the teasing in her tone. "I couldn't say anything conspicuous in case the bug transmitted sound as well as our position. Thanks for doing what I asked. I appreciate it."

"I'm sure you do." Her tone was wry, but he heard

a lilt of humor in her voice. "Next time, before you drive through a garage door you might warn me."

Fire engines with their sirens blaring passed them going the other way.

"Sorry. All I could think about was getting out fast."

"To avoid the fire?"

"Yeah."

"What else?"

She knew him too well, as if she knew he hadn't told her the whole story. But she was entitled to know what he had been thinking. "I drove out fast in case the intruder had a friend waiting outside."

"A friend ready to pick us off?" She sighed. "This was a disaster."

"How so?"

"We almost got caught. We didn't find out enough to tie Leroy to Vince and we're sitting here naked."

"But it was fun, and naked isn't so bad when you consider the alternatives." He kept his eyes on the road and tried to keep a grin off his face. "Besides, we learned a lot."

"We did?"

"Sure. This operation has just become much more interesting."

"Because we're naked? Really, Jack, I thought you could think of better things to do when you took your clothes off than crashing through garage doors and speeding."

"I'm not speeding." He chuckled. "Your case is more complicated than I figured. Someone is trying to hide evidence that would prove you didn't take any bribes—and they're desperate."

"Seems to me we're the ones who are desperate. My house keys were in my fanny pack. And I don't fancy ringing my parents' doorbell dressed in my birthday suit."

"Don't sweat it. We aren't going to your house."

"Why not?"

"We don't want anyone following us. Someone planted that bug on you. We have to assume they know where to find you at your folks' house."

In his rearview mirror Jack noted the police car on his tail. He checked then double-checked his speedometer.

Piper picked up on the black and white following them. "Damn it, Jack. Are you speeding?"

"No."

The cop car flashed lights and siren.

"Then why is he pulling us over?"

"My guess is that I smashed out my taillights on the garage door." He stepped on the gas.

"What are you doing?"

"Protecting you."

She glanced at the speedometer that was already up to ninety miles per hour. "Protecting me? At this speed, you're more likely to get me killed."

Jack eased off the gas, just a tad. "You want me to stop? I'll stop. But let me remind you that neither of us has identification and that we'll be arrested for indecent exposure. The choice is yours."

DAMN. DAMN. DAMN.

Tonight had been a disaster. Not only had the plan to do away with Donovan and Payne failed, they'd found the bug that ordinary civilians would never have discovered.

Although the idea of them running through the night naked could have been amusing, that they had disposed of the tracking and listening device was a major setback.

Think. You know what they want. You know where they are going.

Eventually they would find Leroy. Leroy could be the key to ending this series of mistakes.

A message flashed on the computer screen and the program automatically decrypted the terse sentence.

"We cannot do business until you solve your problem. Take care of it."

Just great. The deal of the century going down the drain. But that wouldn't happen.

Tomorrow they would die.

Chapter Five

Piper had always thought that if she ever took her clothes off for Jack, they'd make wild passionate love—not be a hairbreadth from being arrested.

"Do you think the arsonist called in our license plate number or the make and model of the car to the police?"

"I doubt it. We left too fast. It was dark. And arsonists don't usually think of calling the cops to pinch-hit for them."

Jack had a point. She, too, doubted that the police had a reason to connect them to the fire. And she didn't want him to stop the car. She'd already suffered enough humiliation with the department over her firing. If they were stopped by the cops, she'd probably know the officer, and he or she might let her go—but she'd be a laughingstock. If she ever won her job back, she wouldn't be able to face her co-workers. And besides, the Clearwater police department had a no-chase policy unless the offenders had committed a felony and were considered dangerous to the public.

"Okay, Jack. Speed up, carefully." Now in addition to getting her naked, he'd reduced her to talking in oxymorons. Speed killed. Every cop knew that. At least at this time of night the roads were relatively empty, and Jack was a professional behind the wheel.

Jack stepped on the gas, and she steadfastly refused to look at the speedometer. Instead she watched telephone poles blur past, and watched the flashing lights recede into the distance.

"You okay?" Jack asked.

"Sure, I'm just peachy. In one night I've broken in to and entered a private citizen's house, escaped burning to death in an arson fire that I may get blamed for starting, and run from the police—not to mention…"

"Not to mention?"

"Nothing." She would not admit to him how insulted she was that he had barely looked at her. Jack, the biggest woman chaser of all time, had no interest in her when she was sitting next to him without a stitch of clothing. She wasn't embarrassed, but angry. What was wrong with her? She knew she wasn't Britney Spears, but she was attractive. The old joke flashed in her head that all it took to please a man was to show up naked with beer. But if Jack needed a buzz to want her—then the fault was his.

What was wrong with him?

Surely if he had a woman in his life, he would have brought her with him on vacation? She glanced at him. He'd turned off the dash lights, but streetlights occasionally shone in and she glimpsed his sex, erect and jutting. Ah, he *did* want her—at least physically. So why was he holding back?

"Jack, are you hooked up with anyone special?"

He shook his head. "Why?"

"Just wondering."

"Why?"

"Just wondering if you have to explain our current clothesless situation to anyone," she lied, unwilling to point out to him she'd clearly seen what was pointing up from his lap.

"That reminds me." Jack dialed his cell phone.

Surprised, she frowned at him. "Who are you calling in the middle of the night?"

"My boss."

"He won't appreciate being awakened—"

"He doesn't sleep."

"Everyone sleeps."

"What's up, Jack?" Logan Kincaid had a deep sexy voice—an American version of Sean Connery, husky, manly and alert—that practically sizzled through the speaker phone. He certainly didn't sound as if he'd been sleeping, but rather as if he'd been interrupted from a dinner party.

"I've got you on speaker phone, and I'm with Piper Payne," Jack said, and his polite way of letting his boss know their conversation wasn't private intrigued her.

Piper spoke up. "Hello, Mr. Kincaid. Thanks for taking my case."

"No problem. Please call me Logan. Is Jack treating you all right?"

She looked at Jack and grinned. "Actually, he made me take off all of my clothes."

"That's why I was calling." Jack inserted himself into the conversation without missing a beat.

Logan chuckled. "You need instructions about what to do next?"

"It's not like that. We're in my car. I just eluded the police." Jack explained what had happened at Leroy's house.

Logan didn't hesitate. "Go to the private airport. I'll have clothes, cash and additional equipment waiting in the chopper."

"The lady's a size eight, 36C. Shoe size, seven. Oh, and we need fake ID."

So Jack had noticed her body, and he'd gotten her measurements exactly right. She wasn't sure whether to be flattered or annoyed.

"Give me an hour."

"Thanks, Boss."

"And I'm going to send a file over to Adam Knight. That okay with you?"

"Sure. We can use all the help we can get."

"Right now Adam's helping Kirk Hardaker on another case, so he may not get back to you immediately."

Jack ended the connection.

"Who's Adam Knight?" she asked.

"An expert profiler and new member of the Shey

Group. One of the best in the business. I've seen him nail a criminal's background, right down to how his mother treated him when he was a baby. The guy's good. Amazing, really.''

"I think you're amazing."

Jack didn't say a word. He didn't look at her, just kept driving.

"Jack."

"Yeah."

"We've got an hour to kill."

"Yeah."

An hour in the car with Jack. Her pulse raced at the thought. As a teen, she'd always wanted to lose her virginity to Jack. She'd put that down to a crush, and she hadn't been ready back then. She was more than ready now. He was the most experienced guy she knew. He'd take care of her—make sure her first time was good.

But he would never make the first move, not when he kept calling her Pest, clinging to some little-sister image from the past. She would have to say something to indicate her willingness. But what? She had never thought saying a few simple words would be so enormously difficult.

But she might never have a better opportunity.

Say something.

Her tongue almost refused to cooperate, but she forced out the words. "We could make the most of the hour."

He didn't pretend to misunderstand. "Not a good idea."

"Why not?"

Even in the dark, she could see the irritation on his face. "Because I don't keep condoms in my glove compartment."

If he thought he could discourage her so easily, he didn't know her well. "We could at least park by the beach and get to know one another better. A few kisses, a little touching, stroking, caressing. Some friendly exploration…"

"No." He practically growled his refusal.

"You don't find me attractive?"

"I wouldn't be male if I didn't find you attractive."

"So what's the problem?"

"We need to keep moving."

Was he making excuses to avoid her? Because he really wasn't interested? Or for some other reason?

She placed her hand on his warm bare shoulder. He flinched and swerved, then jerked the car back into their lane.

"Stop that."

She let her fingers trace tiny circles on his shoulder. "We could be good together, don't you think?"

"No. I don't think."

"So you never mix business with pleasure?"

He brushed her hand off his shoulder. "I don't mix pleasure and you."

He really was cute when he was annoyed. No wonder she'd gotten such a kick out of pestering him as a kid. It was even more fun now. She placed her hand on his bare knee, enjoyed the feel of his muscles tensing.

Jack swore. Long and loud and using words in several languages she didn't even recognize. "Haven't you ever heard that *no* means *no*?"

She laughed. "No only means *no* when the woman says it."

"That's sexist," he complained.

"Come on, Jack. When was the last time you said no to a willing woman?"

He cursed some more.

"That wasn't an answer."

"I care about you, Pest. We grew up together."

So that was his excuse? He still thought she was a kid? She let her voice go husky, realizing that flirting with Jack was not only fun, but a great way to let off steam. "I'm all grown up now." She shimmied just a little in her seat. "Or haven't you noticed?"

"Must you do that?" Jack practically growled at her. It was bad enough that Piper didn't have clothes on. Worse still that she wanted to make love, and he couldn't think of one good reason to refuse her that wouldn't insult her. Jack didn't have many rules in his life, but he did have one. He didn't do virgins. Ever. He liked his women experienced and knowing the score. And since Piper had hinted that she was still a virgin, her innocence was more than enough to set him running in the opposite direction, except he'd committed to helping her clear her name.

How the hell had he gotten into this mess? He was supposed to be on vacation, hitting the beach and the sack with some eager *and experienced* stranger. Instead he was trapped with the girl next door—who oh-so-obviously was no longer a girl, but a full-grown woman with sex on her mind.

"Must I do what?" she asked.

"Jiggle."

"You needn't insult me." She sounded prim and proper and hurt, but he knew better than to apologize. He much preferred that she think him a slimeball. Then she wouldn't encourage a certain uncontrollable part of his anatomy to demand more than its fair share of his blood supply. It wasn't as if he could sit on his erection and hide his reaction to her.

He threaded a hand through his hair and grimaced at the irony. He couldn't remember the last time he'd said no to a luscious, ripe, willing female over the age of consent. But he would do so now. Somehow. And if holding back made him ornery and grumpier than his usual lovable self, she would just have to put up with him.

"Jack."

"Now what?"

"How much gas do we have?"

"Enough." No way would he turn on the dash lights.

"So how is Logan getting us fake ID?"

Jack liked this subject much better. Maybe business would distract him. "Logan knows the right people."

"But he doesn't know what I look like."

"One of our team members can hack into the Department of Motor Vehicles' computer system with one hand tied behind his back. Ryker will get your real photograph and Logan will dub it onto your new ID."

She didn't say a word. "What?" he asked.

"I'm trying to count how many laws we're breaking."

"You need to look at this as self-defense."

"Right. Hacking into the Department of Motor Vehicles is self-defense."

"It is if the fake ID saves your life."

"It's my reputation that's in danger, not my life," she argued.

"Have you forgotten that someone followed us to Leroy's house and tried to burn us alive?"

"I haven't forgotten. But we don't have one shred of evidence that anyone knew we were there."

"Have you forgotten the tracking device? You heard it beeping."

"I heard beeps. I have only your word what caused those beeps."

"So you think it was a coincidence that an arsonist started that fire in Leroy's house just when we happened to be there?"

"We have no evidence."

That was the police officer in her talking. No doubt the department had drilled into her that she couldn't put criminals away without a legal chain of admissible evidence. But sometimes the Shey Group had to use other methods to complete their missions. "Look, we'll get your evidence."

Piper leaned forward and pressed the button to open the glove compartment.

"Don't."

He spoke too late. The box popped open and the tiny light inside came on, illuminating his spare gun, a map of Florida and a box of condoms. "Well, well. So not only have you taken up a criminal lifestyle—"

"I'm not a criminal."

"—you're a liar, too. I believe the last man who used those exact words was President Nixon—right before he resigned."

Piper removed the gun, checked the load and held the gun by her leg.

"Expecting trouble?" Jack asked, refusing to apologize when he'd only been trying to protect her.

"One never knows what kind of snake might be lurking just around the next corner...or be sitting right next to me."

He deserved that. However, he had no intention of defending himself. Her anger at his lie would prevent her from flirting with him.

So her next comment took him aback. "You wanted me to find those condoms, didn't you?"

"Excuse me? I didn't know you were going to open the glove compartment."

"You want me angry at you." She spoke aloud, ignoring his protest, but almost as if she was figuring him out as she went along. "Are you afraid of me, Jack?"

Damn. Damn. Damn. He didn't want to go there. Now was not the time for self-analysis. He preferred to keep things simple. He'd always protected Piper, and he would continue to do so. Period. The sooner he finished this case, the sooner they could part ways. End of story.

He killed his headlights and drove into the airport. His internal clock told him he'd driven around long enough to give Logan the hour he'd needed to make arrangements. Logan had contacts in every part of the world. The man's PalmPilot, locked in a safe inside his office, contained the names and phone numbers of Supreme Court judges, CIA agents, cops, criminals, spies, test pilots, lawyers and doctors, even a Navajo chief. Logan's influence reached from NASA to the White house to the Kremlin. He knew the names of maids, drivers, chefs, ex-marines and bank presidents, many who owed the Shey Group favors. Jack just hoped that this pro bono operation hadn't drawn undue attention.

Hopefully, no one had followed them. But Jack preferred not to take any chances. And since Piper was comfortable with a weapon, he didn't hesitate to leave her behind.

He parked the car behind a fuel shed and turned off the motor. He left the keys in the ignition. "Stay here."

"Wait."

"What? You want me to kiss you goodbye?"

She ignored his sarcasm. "What do I do if you don't come back?"

"You get out fast. Then hit the redial button on my cell and call Logan for help."

"Okay."

Jack slipped out of his seat.

"Jack."

"What?"

"Be careful, okay?"

"Yeah."

"Jack."

"Now what?"

Her tone was whispered, yet husky. "Would it really kill you to kiss me goodbye?"

By the lilt in her tone he knew she was teasing him again. He shook his head and headed toward the helicopter, but he still heard her say, "You have no idea what you're missing."

Great. He didn't need to think about kissing her. This pickup might or might not be dangerous. However, until he knew what or who was waiting out there for him, he needed to keep his wits about him.

Jack didn't rush. He merged into the deep shadows of an airplane, stopped and listened. Crickets chirped. Frogs croaked. And the balmy Gulf breeze seemed to mock him.

He zigzagged toward the helicopter.

PIPER NEEDED THE TIME away from Jack to get her thoughts together. She'd never acted so boldly before.

What was happening to her to cause her to flirt so brazenly with Jack? She'd dated before, of course, but she'd never been serious with anyone. And she'd never come on to a guy as she had with Jack. But with him, flirting came spontaneously, and she'd forgotten that she was a twenty-five-year-old virgin pretending to be a more experienced woman.

Exchanging banter with Jack was fun and came more naturally to her than she'd ever believed possible. It was almost as if being freed from the rules and regulations of a police officer's life had opened up new possibilities she'd never seen before.

And she liked Jack. Trusted him in a way that surprised her. It must have to do with their history. Although she'd pestered Jack unmercifully through the years, he'd always been kind to her. And when the chips were down he'd always protected her, charging to her rescue before she'd even thought to ask for his help.

So now she trusted him enough to want him to take her virginity—only, he'd said he didn't want her.

Yeah, right.

However inexperienced she might be, she'd have to have been blind not to have seen the part of his anatomy that had told a different story.

However, Jack seemed to have his own agenda— one that didn't include knowing her intimately.

After so many years of waiting to make love, she shouldn't be impatient now. She'd never been one to go gaga over some guy. She'd always been practical. And she'd never been in lust.

Until now. Perhaps being naked had stimulated her hormones. Perhaps it was being naked with Jack. She only knew she longed to touch him and have him touch her.

But Jack had refused her with a grumpiness that told her saying no hadn't been so easy for him. *Good.* Time would work in her favor. She'd wear down his resistance and, without another woman for him to turn to, she'd be willing to bet her badge—if she still had it— that the Jack Donovan she knew and wanted in her bed wouldn't hold out against her wishes for all that long.

He'd been gone only a few minutes, but the seconds had ticked away like days. Despite his competence and the gun in his hand, she couldn't help being concerned.

His last instructions notwithstanding, she wouldn't drive off and leave him here. Not when she had a loaded gun.

"Psst. It's me." Jack stepped out of the shadows fully clothed in a dark shirt, skintight jeans and shoes.

"Any problems?" she asked, feeling more naked now that he was dressed and she wasn't. How ridiculous. Irrational. And she was glad the darkness hid her nipples, which had suddenly pebbled into hard buds.

"Went off without a hitch—" he scratched his ankle "—except that I have a few ant and mosquito bites."

"You okay?"

"The sting's not that bad." Without looking her way, he tossed a duffel bag into her lap. "Help yourself."

Jack turned his back, although why she couldn't be sure, since he'd already seen everything she had to offer. He had to be more affected by her than he pretended, or he wouldn't be so set on keeping his distance.

One thing she knew about Jack was his taste in women. He liked them easygoing and easy to say goodbye to. So maybe, just maybe, he had feelings for her that scared him away from seeing her as a woman rather than a pesky little kid.

With a sigh she pulled out a sweatshirt. Too hot for that. She found a soft cotton T-shirt and jeans, a bra and panties. Everything smelled brand-new and fit perfectly. Even the sneakers.

"I'm dressed."

Jack motioned her to follow him. She placed his gun in her duffel along with the box of condoms from the glove compartment. Jack stowed their belongings and a laptop inside the trunk of a two-door white BMW.

"Wow. Your boss sure does things first-class."

"We don't need to risk being pulled over because of broken taillights." He handed her a soft leather purse. "You'll find new identification with your driver's license and social security card inside. You should memorize the new information.''

"Is a fake ID really necessary?"

"I don't know who or what we're up against yet." He slipped back into the driver's seat. "I've reserved two rooms for us at the beach."

He placed a slight emphasis on the word *two*.

"Adjoining rooms?" she asked, more to bug him than because she wanted to know.

"No." He revved the engine and pulled out of the private airport. "But I'm right next door."

"In case I need you?" she teased.

"Right."

"So you can comfort me if I have any nightmares?"

"No, so I can spank you if you misbehave."

She could have sworn he'd blushed. Too bad there wasn't more light so she could be certain. Curious, she glanced at him. "Are you into that kind of thing?"

"I was kidding."

"So then why are you blushing?"

"Oh, for the love of…" He'd been driving under the speed limit, his body relaxed, even with her hazing. But he suddenly stiffened, his head snapping up, his foot pressing down on the gas.

"What's wrong?"

"We've picked up a tail. Let's hope this airport has a security guard who is curious about our presence."

"We haven't done anything wrong. Why are you speeding again?"

"Because I'm not sure who's back there, or how they found us."

"You want me to take off my clothes again?"

"No."

"Why don't you spin around so we can find out who's back there?"

"Not while you're with me."

She didn't bother keeping the irritation from her voice. "While I'm with you? What's that supposed to mean?"

"Logan would have my ass if I led a client into danger."

"And you always obey your boss's orders?"

Jack chuckled. "Damn straight."

She didn't believe him. "More likely you're careful not to get caught breaking Logan's rules."

"He doesn't have many, and he trusts the men who work for him."

She snorted. "He trusts *you*?"

"Those are fighting words, woman."

"In less than two hours you've already lied to me once. About the condoms that you *don't* keep in your glove compartment."

Jack swung a hard left. "Can you nag me later? I'm a little busy right now."

"How convenient," she muttered. Naturally Jack chose not to hear her. He'd sounded insulted when she'd claimed he wasn't trustworthy. *Good*. She liked getting under his skin. She liked touching his skin even better. And decided that the best way to wear down his resistance was to touch him often.

With another driver she might have been concerned over the car behind them, but she had no doubts that Jack would lose the other car. He had the nerves of a high-stakes poker player and the instincts of a NASCAR driver. However, if she'd been making the decisions, she would have been more inclined to find out who was following them.

But maybe she was too close to the situation. She wanted a quick solution to her problem, so she could move on with her life. Any decision she made would be based as much on emotion as logic.

Being fired from the police force wasn't like being fired from most other jobs. For one thing, no other police department would hire her unless they were desperate. But the worst was that cops were tight with one another, serving as both family and friends. They shared a sense of community and closeness that she missed more than she had ever thought she would.

So it was only natural for her to turn to Jack for comfort and friendship. And separate rooms or not, she intended to sleep next to him tonight.

Chapter Six

When the car behind them had made a U-turn and headed back into the airport, Jack had relaxed. Almost positive that the vehicle was simply airport security, he'd still driven a circuitous route before parking at the beachfront motel he'd chosen because they'd remodeled last year and boasted a high-speed Internet connection in their advertisements. And the laptop Logan had provided could access the more complex computer system back at the Payne house.

Piper reached for the cell phone he'd placed in the console between them. "I need to call my parents."

"Not a good idea."

"Why?"

"Their phone is probably tapped, and if you call, we might be traced here."

"Look, if I don't show up by tomorrow morning, my parents will be frantic with worry. I can't do that to them, and besides, they'll undoubtedly report me as a missing person. Knowing Mom, by tomorrow afternoon my face will be plastered all over the news."

He placed his hand over hers. "Can you talk for less than ten seconds?"

"Sure."

"There's another way to get a message to them tonight."

"Without sending smoke signals?"

"We'll reroute through a third party. Bounce the signal from satellite to satellite."

"You can do that through a cell phone?"

"Think about what you want to say. The call will cut off automatically within twelve seconds to avoid any possibility of a trace."

He dialed about twenty numbers into his cell phone. During his career with the Shey Group he'd often used this tactic. The codes he pressed routed the call through twenty cities, five time zones and four satellites, but when her father answered the phone his voice came through loud and clear over the speaker. "Hello."

"Dad, didn't want you to worry. I'll be gone for a few days. Give my love to Mom?"

"Sure. You okay?"

"I'm good. Love you."

"Love you, too." She clicked the phone off with five seconds to spare.

Logan glanced at her. "You sure that's going to be enough to reassure them?"

"My parents always ask if I'm okay when I call in from a date or am out late. *I'm good* is our code."

"What does it mean?"

"I'm fine, having a good time."

"And if you want to indicate otherwise?"

"I say, *I'm good to go.* That means I want to come home, and Dad would think up some emergency and demand that I be back home soon."

"That works?"

"Like a charm. I haven't had to use it often, but no guy wants the entire police department out hunting him."

"I didn't realize your folks were that protective."

"Mom always worried about my safety, more so after the fire that burned our house down. And as a college professor, Dad knows too much about randy teenage boys and their raging hormones."

Jack popped the trunk and removed their luggage. "I'm surprised they let you even talk to a wild kid like me."

"They didn't worry because...you weren't interested." She said the words lightly. "However, they might spend a sleepless night if they knew we'd just spent several hours together naked."

Her words sent heat straight to his groin, and he stifled a groan. Did she *have* to keep reminding him how great she looked without her clothes? Of course, she looked good in her clothes, too. Hell, she looked good, period. Good enough to dream about—especially when she'd made it quite clear that she would welcome him into her room, her bed, her arms.

Jack almost demanded that the desk clerk give them rooms at opposite ends of the motel. But he couldn't do that in good conscience. While he didn't believe she was in danger, he might be wrong.

Just the way he'd been wrong about his being able to think about her the same way he used to—as a kid. A pest. Like the little sister he'd never had.

She'd grown up on him, but in some ways she hadn't changed at all. She still enjoyed pestering him, and she still knew how to press his hot buttons. Only, now she didn't just irritate and exasperate—she also titillated, tempted and tantalized him with a sexy honesty that left him on edge.

He needed a drink. He needed a woman. Any woman but her. Since that wasn't going to happen, he had only one solution—he intended to work through what was left of the night.

They each entered their rooms. Through the thin walls he could hear her moving around, taking a shower. While he set up the laptop and checked the progress of Ryker's program back at the Payne house, he tried not to think about the water sluicing over her tanned skin or the not-so-tanned parts where her swimsuit kept her flesh white and creamy. The contrast had automatically drawn his gaze to her breasts and he'd had to fight to keep his eyes focused on the road. But now he could imagine her back arching as she raised her arms to wash her hair. As she tipped up her face to the water, it would slide down over her, caressing and stroking the tempting flesh that he wouldn't allow himself to touch.

The words in the files on the screen in front of him blurred.

Concentrate.

Working was futile. How could he think when his imagination wouldn't let go? He envisioned the water droplets trickling down her cheek and sliding over her neck to the tips of her rosy breasts. He would delicately lick the nipple, and she would thread her fingers through his hair, tug him closer.

Damn.

He slapped the laptop screen down. No point in trying to work. No point in avoiding the fact that his body was as sexually charged as he'd ever been.

Since he had no intention of satisfying his urges—not with Piper—he had only a few alternatives. Physical exhaustion might do the trick. A run on the beach would take off this edge, then a long swim back should cool him down.

Except he didn't want to leave her alone. The danger might be minimal, but he couldn't take the risk.

He changed out of his jeans and shirt into loose running shorts that could double as a swimsuit—not that he expected to meet many people, unless they were awake to watch the sun rise in a couple of hours. There was no reason he couldn't jog back and forth on the beach, never going out of shouting range.

Jack stepped through a sliding glass door that faced the beach. A light breeze wafted across the still waters of the Gulf, which lapped gently on the powdered sand. A crescent moon, a very bright Venus and a dull, red-hued Mars lit the early-morning sky.

He breathed in the salty air that reminded him of home. When he was away on a mission he always thought of home—not the house where he and his parents had lived, but the beach. The beach was where he'd come to eat and swim and play. He also liked the quiet moments like this where he could think.

He'd always dreamed of traveling across oceans, visiting other continents and experiencing other cultures. But this beach couldn't be beaten for the dreams it represented. Dreams he'd accomplished—almost every one.

Despite his parents' belief that he was a spendthrift, Jack was set for life. He needn't ever work again if he chose not to. But he had great friends, a career he loved. So why was he feeling edgy and as though he could do so much more if only he opened himself to new experiences and possibilities?

As experienced as Jack was with women, he didn't think much could surprise him anymore. Yet his attraction to Piper had him startled by its intensity. He decided to put it down to forbidden fruit—greener pastures that couldn't be explored.

If necessary, he could deal with the sexual frustration on his own. But the emotional side of this attraction left him almost shell-shocked. The surfacing of protective urges that he hadn't known he had sent him for a loop. Jack usually looked out for Jack and his team. He risked his life on missions, often without even knowing the people under fire that he flew in to save.

With Piper, he could recall her every expression. Shock as her eyes widened after he said something outrageous. Amusement as her mouth turned up. Mischievousness as her eyes brightened when she teased him. But it was the heat in her emerald eyes, the passion she offered, that almost did him in.

Jack wasn't the right type of guy for a woman like Piper. He worked hard and played hard, and in between, he didn't have room in his life to make another person happy. If Piper didn't know this basic fact about him, he did.

Protecting her from himself was ludicrous. If the guys on his team could see him right now, they'd never let him hear the end of it. Because Jack did what felt good. Jack took the easy way in and out of bed—and he never looked back, never had regrets. As he pounded up and down the beach, his body breaking into a sweat, he wanted to blame the fact that he and Piper had been childhood friends for his protective feelings now. And he almost convinced himself.

Even now, instead of settling into a slow and easy jog, he pushed his body, anxious to tire himself quickly—just so he could get back to her and make sure she was safe. He plunged into the warm Gulf water, but swam only a few yards. He needed to stay close—in case she needed him.

With a disgusted curse, he rose from the water and

headed back to his room. To find her curled up and sleeping in the middle of his bed.

"JACK?" PIPER LIFTED her head from the pillow. Jack had come in through the sliding glass door. Half-awake, still rubbing the sleep from her eyes, she thought he looked like a sea god with his bare chest and muscular legs, his hair slicked back.

"What are you doing here, Pest?"

"I must have fallen asleep."

He grabbed a towel from around his neck and dried his face. He looked chiseled from granite, his face hard with attitude, his body larger than life, his eyes dark blue chips of ice. "You haven't answered my question."

He didn't look happy to see her. In fact, he looked totally unlike the Jack she knew, practically downright hostile.

She stopped rubbing her eyes and stretched. "How was I supposed to sleep with all the beeping coming from your room?"

"What beeping?"

"Your computer was making enough racket to wake the dead. So I came in here to find out what was up."

"How'd you get in?"

"I picked the lock."

"You?"

"One of the criminals I arrested showed me how," she admitted.

"And when you discovered that I wasn't here?"

"Well, the computer stopped making noise, but I thought it might be important, so I decided to stay so I could tell you about it."

"You could have left me a note."

"I thought of that," she admitted. "But I don't like sleeping in a strange bed."

He jerked his thumb at the bed. "This one is just as strange as the one in your room and you had no trouble sleeping here."

"That's because I knew you were coming back." She grinned, knowing it would irritate him almost as much as her answer.

"That is the most illogical, irrational thing you've ever said."

"Oh, really?"

"You aren't making sense."

"Sure I am." She flicked her hair over her shoulder and gave him her best you-can-do-better look. "You just don't *want* to understand."

He gave a disgusted grunt, then fisted his hands on his hips in what she thought of as his tough-guy pose. "Okay. You told me about the beeping. I'll check it later. Right now I'm going to take a shower—"

"Can I watch?" She said the most outrageous thing she could think of just to get deeper under his skin. She hoped he might swat her with the towel or laugh or tease her back. Instead, he blushed again. In the bright light of the room his tanned cheeks definitely turned red this time. Only, she had no idea why.

"Go back to your room, Pest."

"But—"

"Go." He fired the command like a bullet.

"Okay, okay, I'm going." She ambled toward the sliding glass door, and he didn't wait to see if she kept going. He stalked into the bathroom and slammed the door—another most un-Jack-like reaction.

How had she made him blush? What could he be doing in that shower that could have caused him to react like a teenage boy caught with his nose in a *Playboy* centerfold?

Oh, my. Could she really be having that much of an effect on him that Jack had to resort to… Halfway to her room, she turned around. She entered Jack's room and slipped back into his bed. Annoying him as a child had been fun, but annoying him as a woman was positively delicious.

If she'd been bolder, she might have tested the bathroom door to see if he'd locked it behind him. She didn't think he had, but she couldn't summon up the courage to walk in. But she wanted to…because maybe if she caught him off guard, he'd give them what they both wanted.

Jack took a long shower, so long that she thought he must be trying to use up all the motel's hot water. She might have actually fallen asleep again, except that once more his computer began to beep annoyingly.

With a sigh she climbed out of bed and opened the laptop's screen. Surely even she could lower the volume on the desktop, so the beeping wouldn't get them kicked out of the motel. It was a wonder that the people on the other side hadn't complained.

She didn't recognize any of the symbols on the desktop. He didn't use Windows, but an operating system that she was totally unfamiliar with.

When Jack exited the bathroom with a towel around his hips and saw her, he rolled his eyes toward the ceiling. A smile played at the corner of his mouth. Apparently his "shower" had calmed his irritation with her.

She'd just have to heat him up again. But first she wanted answers about the infernal beeping machine. "Doesn't this thing have an off button?"

Jack reached over her shoulder and hit a function key. The beeping stopped.

"Thanks." She realized he thought she'd returned because of the beeping. Well, she'd let him continue to think so for a while. "So why is it beeping and, please, don't tell me the battery is low."

"Can't." He pointed to an electric socket. "I've got it plugged in to electricity."

"Did it find something about my case?"

Jack pulled up a chair and began to type. "Let's have a look."

"WELL, WHAT DID the program find?" Piper asked, obviously impatient for answers.

Jack wished he could satisfy her curiosity. As he scrolled through pages of data, he shrugged. "The system has found nothing in common between the two citizens who accused you of bribery.''

Piper frowned at the laptop as if it was at fault. ''Then why was it beeping?''

Jack rubbed his neck. ''It was telling me the search needs new parameters.''

''In English, please.'' She brushed his hands aside and rubbed his sore neck. Her fingers seemed to find the kinks and knots without much trouble, freeing his hands to type on the keyboard.

''The computer hasn't finished searching every clue, but the program is suggesting we are on the wrong track.''

''Does it suggest where to look next?'' she asked sarcastically. He couldn't blame her. He was disappointed, also. But he wasn't ready to give up. Unlike her, he'd seen the program work wonders.

''As a matter of fact—it does.''

''Look, Dad teaches computer science and I've learned enough from him to know that machines don't think.''

Jack bit back a groan as her fingers unkinked a sore spot. ''I told you that the man who designed this program is a genius. He assigned probabilities to different scenarios. And by calculating the odds statistically—''

''Jack.'' She rubbed harder and yawned. ''It's late. Or early.'' She glanced at the light brightening the night sky and heralding a new day. ''Just explain the computer stuff to me in words of less than two or three syllables, if possible.''

He'd give it a try. "The computer's parameters indicate a high probability that—"

"Jack, in English."

"The charges against you were, probably, number one—personal. Number two—made by someone with a grudge. And three—made by someone who is an expert in computer technology or programming."

"I don't know anyone like that. Is the program giving us names to check out?"

"I'm afraid the program is not that specific." Jack typed some more. He could tell that Piper wasn't impressed, but she didn't understand the equations inside the machine. Ryker had programmed each factor to weigh in by using crime statistics from the police, FBI and CIA. Not only could the machine follow a money trail, but it could also tell whether your next-door neighbor—or your brother—was more apt to have an affair with your wife than the mailman was.

"The computer has checked through every felon you put behind bars. Only one of them has the computer skills to pull off a hack into the police department."

She shook her head. "I didn't need the computer for that. His name is Eddie Rickel. I've already checked him out. He doesn't have Internet access in jail."

"Maybe he has a friend on the outside."

"Maybe."

"The computer program believes there is a high

probability that whoever burned down your parents' house and whoever framed you is the same person."

"Oh, come on." She shook her head again. This time she also stopped rubbing and frowned down at him. "I don't see it. One crime was arson and the other takes computer skills."

"Don't forget the fire at Leroy's house tonight." Jack flipped off the screen and straddled his chair, causing her to stop rubbing his neck, a massage he was enjoying all too much and which semidistracted him from fully concentrating. "Did you check your mother's old police cases?"

"Yes. I went through years of files." She sat on the bed opposite him. "They weren't all closed, and I actually took over a few of them after I made detective. But none were computer crimes."

He tried a different tack. "Your father teaches computer science at the university, right?"

"He's had hundreds of students go through his classes. It's impossible to narrow them down, but I checked the ones who failed his courses or might have carried a grudge," she protested. "Besides, why would they want me to be fired?"

"Well, you were unofficially investigating the arson at your folks' house."

"So I was poking around and asking a few questions? Big deal."

"Suppose you were getting too close to figuring out who did it?"

"So they hack into the police computers, convince

two citizens to accuse me of taking a bribe to get me pulled off the case? I'm sure your computer could figure out that scenario isn't too likely.''

"I guess.''

"Besides, I never was close to figuring out who burned down the house. The insurance company and the fire department also looked into it. None of us found anything solid. My regular job kept me too busy to dig very deep.''

"When exactly did the house burn down?'' he asked.

"A year ago. While my parents were on vacation. I was living in an apartment at the time. There doesn't seem to be any connection. Your computer isn't making much sense.''

She sounded so hopeless that Jack would have tried to cheer her up even if he hadn't disagreed. "We just haven't tied all the angles together yet. I want to speak with your father tomorrow. There may be a way to narrow down which students we should talk to.''

"How?''

"Well, for starters, we could find out who is still in the area. And also which students had the capability to hack into the police department. That's not easy. So it would have to be someone brilliant. Advanced students. Someone your father will likely remember.''

"Do you think my folks could be in danger?''

"Let's not jump to conclusions. Have they had any other trouble this past year? Any car accidents? Close calls?''

She shook her head. "I know that you're trying to help, but this seems like a wild-goose chase."

"In my experience, most investigations start out that way. We still need to speak to Leroy and his mistress. We'll keep digging until we get to the bottom of this mystery. Give Ryker's program a chance to work. And once Adam sends us his profile, it should help us narrow down our suspects."

"Jack?"

"What?"

"Do you think I should just move on with my life? Forget about the police department and clearing my name?"

"Give up? That's not like you."

"I just wonder if I'm being dumb for trying to hang on—"

"To a job that you loved? I don't think so. But what I think doesn't matter. What do you want?"

She drew her legs up to her chest under her T-shirt and wrapped her arms around them. Only her toes stuck out, and she curled them under her feet as if withdrawing into herself. He didn't like seeing her so vulnerable. He much preferred to see her sassy, strong. Even pestering him was preferable.

He stood, wanting to go to her and put his arms around her. But she was half-dressed, sitting on his bed. In a motel room. Pure temptation.

No way should he go to her.

He paced. "It's going to be fine."

"Yeah, right."

"We're going to figure out who did this to you and why."

"If you say so." She lifted her head, trying to be brave, and her courage pulled at his heart.

He could not go to her.

"I have a very good track record for solving these kinds of cases."

"Really? I thought you were mostly a pilot."

"I am, but since the Shey Group is a team, I've learned a lot from the best guys in the business. And if we can't succeed on our own, I can call in more experts to help."

"Thanks, Jack."

She looked grateful and vulnerable and adorable.

And somehow he found himself on the bed, gathering her into his arms. She snuggled and placed her cheek against his chest.

He rocked her, enjoying the feel of her. And as the sun brought in the new day, Jack knew that he was meant to be here for her at this moment. Holding her seemed so natural and so right.

And when she tipped up her head to look at him, he didn't know how he could continue to resist her.

Chapter Seven

Piper just knew Jack was about to kiss her. As much as she wanted his lips on hers, and as long as she'd waited to get what she wanted, she had no intention of letting him think he could change his mind on a moment's notice and that she'd simply accept whatever crumbs he planned to give her. Nope. She might want Jack, but she had her pride. Since he'd already refused her advances several times, she now had different standards. Higher standards. He had to want to kiss her as much as she wanted to kiss him, and no way could he possibly be as needy—since the thought appeared to have just occurred to him.

He could wait. And if that meant she had to wait, too—so be it.

She went from cuddly to businesslike by scooting away from him, standing and checking the alarm clock. "If we hurry, we can catch my dad at the coffee shop before his morning classes."

The look on Jack's face? Priceless. His lower jaw actually hung open before he snapped his mouth closed so hard his teeth snicked together. His lips thinned, but just for a moment before his mouth lifted into a wry grin. But it was the respect gleaming in his eyes that told her that while her female instincts might not include experience, they worked just fine, thank you very much.

They packed everything into the trunk of their car and checked out of the motel. Her dad's schedule was as predictable as the school calendar. He taught Monday through Thursday from eight in the morning until noon during summer sessions, which were shorter and more intense. And before starting his day with his students, he fortified himself with breakfast and the sharing of news and local gossip with his coffee klatch— a group of men who'd been meeting at the local shop for years.

She dressed in the new clothes Logan Kincaid had supplied, and met Jack by his car. He had the stereo blasting, which was fine with her, since she didn't feel compelled to talk.

If her father was surprised to see his daughter and Jack arrive together after she hadn't come home last night, he hid his feelings well. However, since she'd overheard her parents discussing her private life one night a few weeks ago, she knew they were concerned, not just by the loss of her job, but that she had no steady guy in her life—and never had. So perhaps her father was relieved that his twenty-five-year-old daughter had finally spent the night with a man—although nothing had happened, if she didn't count riding around naked.

Her father was sitting alone. His friends were paying their bills at the register by the door, but he was finishing up his coffee and the sports page. When he saw them enter, he closed his newspaper and stood.

She hurried to him and gave him a hug, enjoying the scent of bacon, eggs and coffee as well as his favorite cologne. Since he was her height, she had no trouble kissing his cheek. Dressed in slacks and a white shirt, he regarded her from behind gold-rimmed glasses, his twinkling green eyes reminding her of her own.

"Hi, Dad." She released him. "You remember Jack Donovan?"

"Of course." Her father shook Jack's hand. His expression was both warm and wary, as if he hadn't made up his mind what he thought about his only child spending the night with Jack.

One of the reasons she loved her father was that he always backed her up, and he never jumped to conclusions. Fair-minded and even tempered, he might be slow to make a decision, but once he did, it would be a fair one.

"Mr. Payne." Jack spoke quietly. "Sorry to disturb your breakfast."

"Call me Dan." He gestured for them to take seats at his table. "And this isn't a disruption, but a welcome surprise."

"Dad, Jack is trying to help me get my job back."

Her father raised his brows. "I told your mother you wouldn't give up." He nodded at Jack. "So how can I help?"

Jack spoke quietly and succinctly. "My firm has a sophisticated computer program that is suggesting there may be a connection between the arsonist who set fire to your home and whoever has framed your daughter. Since police computer records were hacked, we were hoping you could fill us in on some of your students."

"Hmm. That's one mighty smart computer program you have there. Wouldn't mind taking a look at it."

"I'm sorry. It's classified."

Her father shrugged. "Well, I'm not surprised by the program's theory."

"You're not?" Piper had thought the computer's scenario far-fetched, but she hadn't wanted to insult Jack or the man who'd written the program, whom he so admired. She'd remained silent on the subject, but with her father agreeing, she perked up. Perhaps they were on the right trail, after all.

Her father spoke slowly, as if thinking aloud. "I never suspected that our house might have been burned down by a student—until now. The police told me that the fire was probably started by a neighborhood kid making trouble, or possibly by the family member of someone my wife had put into jail during her career."

"Why do you think differently now, Dad?"

"Mind you, I don't have any proof."

"But you have a theory," she prodded.

He hesitated, but then spoke with sadness. "Six months before the fire, the university computer system suffered a massive virus attack—total corruption of the system. There was chaos. Students couldn't get their grades. Professors couldn't teach their online classes. The university president asked me to track down the culprit—a culprit who knew how to get past the school's fire walls."

"You suspected a student?" Jack asked.

"An advanced student. Someone going for their Ph.D. Or a professor." Her father leaned forward in his chair. "While others repaired the damage in record time, I traced the initial problem to an e-mail."

"Which was bounced from country to country?" Jack guessed.

"You got it."

"So you never found the criminal?" she asked.

"Not exactly."

Piper frowned at her father. "What does that mean?"

"Well, the hacker left a long trail to follow. I got stuck in Bulgaria. They aren't too cooperative over there, but I finally traced the hack back to a major Internet service provider in the United States, which would have eventually led me to the criminal."

"But?" she pressed, sensing his reluctance.

"I backed off."

"Why?"

"The university hadn't suffered as much damage as

they first thought. The system basically needed reformatting and rebooting. We were back up and running within two days. Although the damage wasn't that bad, the climate at the university was nasty and vindictive.''

Piper sighed. ''And you suspected one of your students did this?''

''Yeah. Since I teach the upper-level classes, chances are the virus came from one of my students.'' Her father always had been a softy. On the rare occasion when Piper had needed disciplining, her mother had been the one to do it. And Dad always backed his students, just as he'd always stood up for her. Piper could understand how difficult it would have been for him to turn one of them over to the authorities—especially when he knew they'd be expelled and possibly jailed. But he'd kept this information even from her during her arson investigation. ''And I hated the idea of a student's entire life being ruined for what may have been a prank,'' he added, confirming her suspicions.

Jack frowned. ''I don't understand how this may be connected to the fire, sir.''

''I recorded on a disk every e-mail anyone had sent to the school during the time period in question. If I'd given the disk to the authorities, they could have eventually traced the virus back to the hacker.''

Piper sighed. ''You kept the disk, didn't you?''

''And I warned every class, especially those going

for advanced degrees, that if there was a repeat oc-
currence, I'd turn over the disk to the FBI."

Jack kept his voice low, but he put the puzzle pieces
together before she did. "You kept the disk at home?"

Her father nodded, his face grim. "But I couldn't
believe that the guilty student would burn down the
house to get rid of the evidence on the disk."

"You never made a backup?" Piper asked.

Her father shook his head. "I suppose I should have
told you this as soon as we realized a hacker was behind your career trouble. But I never connected the
two incidents."

"And you never traced the e-mail through the ISP
to the source?"

"I didn't want to know." Her father took Piper's
hand. "However, I never suspected the culprit would
burn down our house or come after you. I still don't
understand why…"

"There could be lots of reasons." Jack ticked them
off. "Revenge and fear top my list."

"Fear?" Piper looked at him in confusion.

He looked straight at her. "Fear that Detective Piper
Payne might catch the arsonist. You were nosing
around the case."

"But I had no leads."

"Yeah, but the hacker didn't know that. Maybe during your investigation you questioned him or her.
Maybe the student has graduated and is now a solid
citizen with a lot to lose—family, a job, a reputation
in the community."

"So out of fear this ex-student got two citizens to frame me?" She sighed. "Your theory sounds far-fetched. For all we know, the computer is wrong and the arson had nothing to do with my being fired."

"Maybe," Jack agreed, but she could see that he didn't think so, and neither did her father. Jack now faced him. "Sir, it's more important than ever for you to give us the names of those students."

"Okay." Her father neatly folded his paper and tucked it to the side of his plate. "Although some students stood out more than others, I can't possibly remember every one. I teach a lot of kids every semester."

A waitress came over, took their orders and poured them each a cup of coffee. Piper hadn't realized how hungry she was until she found herself ordering a three-egg Western omelette with a side of bacon and a glass of orange juice. Staying up all night with Jack had a way of making her hungry—and for more than food.

Even as Jack settled into a conversation with her father, he looked sexy in his crisp white T-shirt and jeans. He had a warm way about him, edgy, with that reckless streak just under the surface that called to her on levels she didn't quite understand.

But she wanted to. She wanted to challenge his restless streak to come out in bed. She wanted a taste of that excitement. It wasn't like Jack to hold back, but she knew he would succumb to the tension simmering between them. And had no doubt that together they would make magic.

Jack helped himself to four packets of sugar, which he poured into his coffee. "We're probably interested in someone you do remember," he told her father. "Someone capable of hacking into the police department. Someone brilliant. Possibly antisocial. Possibly with a military background."

Her father rubbed the bridge of his nose. "Except for the military background, which I wouldn't know about, you're describing about half my students. Can you narrow this down any more?"

"We're probably looking for an older male. Someone who took your upper-level specialized classes during the last five years."

"And someone who still lives in the area," Piper added, knowing her father liked to keep up on his students' careers. She'd interviewed many of his former students when she'd investigated the fire, but none of them had panned out.

"All right." Her father removed his glasses and cleaned them. "The problem with remembering the brilliant ones is that they are usually self-taught and rarely come to class. But I remember several who fit your description. However, bear in mind that I can only guess at their hacking abilities—since that's not a subject I teach."

"Yeah, or Mom might have had to arrest you," Piper teased.

Her father chuckled. "She would have to do her

duty. Even after all these years, your mother has high standards.''

"That's why she chose you."

"Yes. I'm a lucky man. Now, if only I had some grandchildren to teach how to use a keyboard and a mouse,'' he teased Piper right back. She didn't mind. Her parents had made no secret that they'd wanted more than one child. She would have liked a sister or a brother, too. But it hadn't happened.

"Sir, your students…'' Jack prodded, putting the conversation back on track.

Even as a kid she'd suspected that her family's closeness had made Jack sad at the lack in his own family. She wondered if he still felt the lack, or if the new friends that he worked with made up for the void in his past.

Her father wouldn't be rushed. He wiped his lips with a napkin, then settled back in his chair. "First, there's Aaron Hodges. The kid was a computer tycoon before he entered college. He had a thriving business selling souped-up computers before he ever came to the university. In my day the language of youth was overhead cam engines and fuel-injected funny cars. Now kids are into gigahertz, CPUs and megabit-per-second Net connections. That kid would have sold his own grandmother a computer system with a super-cooled micro processor, using a mobo—''

"Dad, you're losing me."

"A mobo is a motherboard. And he would have added a front side bus—''

"Dad."

"An internal electrical pathway to burn through the latest games and whip the online competition."

"Okay. We get the idea. The guy likes speed and gadgets, and would sell them to people who don't need them. What else can you tell us about Aaron?"

"He struck me as an overachiever, a little secretive, maybe willing to break a few rules to get ahead, but that's about it. After he got his undergraduate degree, he left the university for a few years and then returned to get his Ph.D.

Piper wrote Aaron's name down and underlined it. She'd spoken to him. She recalled an ordinary young man with glasses. He'd been more interested in trying to sell her a computer than answering her questions.

"He's one of the best salesmen I've ever met. He now owns Hodges Computer Systems over on Highway 19."

"So he does have assets, as well as a reputation to protect," Piper added. "And the resources to bribe others."

"Who else?" Jack asked.

"I know you said males only, but Danna Mudd was one of the smartest students I've ever taught. She had a double major in computer science and English. And she got kicked out of school for selling term papers to other students."

Piper wrote down her name. She remembered Danna, too, from a phone conversation. She'd struck her as a bright young woman who would go far. "Papers she downloaded off the Internet?"

"Nope. She wrote every word herself."

"Where is she now?" Jack asked.

"I heard she writes grants for one of the charity foundations. Maybe the American Breast Cancer Society. And I also heard that her brother was in the military. Killed in Afghanistan."

Piper bit the end of her pen. Hoping for information about other students, she'd phoned Danna, but had never really considered *her* a suspect. "So she's apparently gone legit and wouldn't want her past hacking coming to light, either."

"We'll check her out," Jack told him.

"And then there was Easy As Pie."

Jack finished his coffee and pushed the cup and saucer aside. "Easy As Pie?"

"His nickname. He was one of those nerdy little kids with the dark glasses that were held together by tape. He had no social skills. He always wore black T-shirts and black baggy pants and a black leather trench coat. Every time I saw him I thought of Columbine High School, but the kid never gave me any problems. I swear he must have dreamed in computer code. And he had a hard time speaking English."

"Was he foreign?" Jack asked.

"No. Just uncommunicative. He was working on some high-speed, ultra super-duper new motherboard. Was going to have it patented. I have no idea if he

succeeded or where he is now. I hope the CIA re-
cruited him, but I'm not sure if he ever graduated.''

''Can you recall his real name?'' Jack asked.

''John Smith.''

''You're kidding.'' Piper looked up from her note
taking. This former student had refused to talk to her
about the fire, telling her through a closed door that
he didn't speak to cops without a lawyer. Since she'd
merely been on a fishing expedition, she'd had no reason to force her way inside or to pull him downtown
for questioning, never mind arrest him.

''Nope, it was John Smith, aka Easy As Pie. I always thought he might have…''

''Might have what?'' Piper asked.

''Been the next Bill Gates or the next Osama bin
Laden. I'm not sure which. The kid had an intensity
about him. Eyes like a fanatic. But I'm not sure if he
had any causes, because he rarely spoke.''

''Thanks, Dad.''

''You're welcome, sweetie. You have any other
leads besides my students?''

He could have said any other long shots, but he
didn't. Obviously her father didn't want to discourage
her, and she loved him for it. He also hadn't said one
word about her whereabouts last night or asked any
embarrassing questions about her and Jack. Yep, she'd
lucked out in the parent department, all right.

''We're checking into the backgrounds of the two
citizens who accused Piper,'' Jack explained to her

dad. "One of them died in a car accident two nights ago."

Her father raised a bushy gray brow. "Accident?"

"That reminds me." Piper wrote a memo to herself on the notepad. "I need to check with the department to see if they've learned anything new."

As their food arrived, her father stood. "I need to get to class, but if I can be of any help, you just let me know."

"Thanks, Dad." She kissed her father goodbye, then dug in to her omelette.

Jack stood and shook her father's hand. "I don't think you need it, but just in case, I'm going to have one of the Shey Group protect your house."

"Thanks. I'll be sure to let my wife know, and you take good care of my girl."

"Yes, sir."

Jack sat back down and eyed Piper's food, then helped himself to a slice of bacon. He gave her a sausage in trade. "You going to eat or call the department?"

"I'm going to eat—before you finish my breakfast for me."

PIPER'S FRIEND INSIDE the police department had the day off, so they'd have to wait another twenty-four hours to hear more on whether Vince's accident had really been an accident. No matter how much Piper tried to cover up her disappointment, he could see frustration in her eyes as they walked out of the café into the parking lot.

Jack had been saving his news for the right time. "The computer found another name for Baby Cakes, Leroy's mistress."

She frowned at him over the roof of the car. "You've been holding back on me?"

"That's what you get for distracting me," he teased. "I was thinking about going to see Ms. Venus De Lux last night—"

"Ms. Venus De Lux?"

"Online she's Baby Cakes. In real life she's a stripper."

"With a name like that, she'd have to be."

"According to her tax return, she works at Club Passion. And she lives in Pelican Bay."

Piper opened the door and slid into the passenger seat. As always, she snapped on her seat belt. "A waterfront address? Pretty fancy digs for a stripper."

"She makes good money, but not that good." Jack inserted the key into the ignition and started the car.

"Let's pay her a visit. Then I want to do a little computer shopping over at Hodges Computer Systems. They probably open at ten. Which should just give us time to talk to Venus first."

"Agreed."

Venus lived inside a luxurious community. Most of the homes were on the intracoastal waterway, but the most extravagant houses sat on the Gulf with their own wide sandy beach and spectacular view.

Jack pulled through an open gate and parked under royal palms beside a sleek Jaguar. Stripping paid well, but not this well. He wondered if her extra income came from Leroy—but Leroy got his cash from his wife.

On the way over, he had thought about the best approach to gaining Venus's cooperation, and had decided to play it by ear. The woman who responded to the doorbell wore a shiny black halter top with pink lace sticking out of the bra, skimpy shorts that showed her navel and fishnet stockings. Her makeup must have been applied with a paintbrush. Obviously she'd just gotten off work. At about five foot six, the auburn-haired woman had big hazel eyes that sparkled with curiosity.

"Venus De Lux?"

"Yes?"

"My name is Jack Donovan and this is Piper Payne. Could we talk to you for a few minutes?"

"I'm not interested in buying any Bibles."

She started to shut the door, but Jack shoved his foot in the crack. "We aren't selling anything, ma'am. We want to talk to you about Leroy."

Venus opened the door wider and frowned at them. "Is he in trouble?"

"Not yet." Jack said nothing more. He simply hoped her curiosity would do the rest.

"All right. Come in. But I'm warning you that I'm not at my best after a hard shift. I danced all last night, and I was just heading to bed. Alone."

"We won't take much of your time," Jack promised, wondering about the emphasis on *alone*. Could Leroy be here? Or was he off on a family vacation as his neighbor had said?

The house's interior was done in black marble and slashes of gold and cream. A pair of ultrahigh heels were next to the front door where she'd kicked them off, probably the moment she'd come home. The interior was neat, albeit a bit gaudy for his taste, but still not what he expected from an exotic dancer.

On stockinged feet Venus led them to a back porch where the Gulf breeze and an overhead fan cooled them. A fountain next to the swimming pool provided a constant background gurgle. "Can I get you anything? Coffee? Iced tea? Bourbon?"

"We just had breakfast. We're fine, thanks."

She poured herself a bourbon and raised the glass. "An after-dinner drink—for me. It was a long night. We have a big South American clientele."

"I used to work nights, too," Piper told her. "But I got fired because Leroy lied about me."

Venus's expression didn't change at Piper's revelation. "You're the cop?"

"Yes."

Jack didn't know if Piper should have admitted that fact so quickly. He suspected that the cops hassled the strip joints as part of their civic responsibility. But Venus didn't seem hostile.

"And I don't understand why Leroy lied about

me," Piper continued. "I was hoping you might know."

Venus swallowed her drink in one gulp, then set the glass down and swirled the ice with a long red nail. "All I can tell you is that he wasn't happy about coming forward."

"What do you mean?" Jack asked.

She shrugged. "It's just a feeling. But I know men. He didn't want his name in the paper. Leroy is a private man. Quiet."

"Do you know if he came into any money recently?" Jack asked.

Venus snorted. "Just the opposite. The guy was broke. All the time. Actually, he owes *me* money." She shook her head. "You'd think I'd know better than to get involved with a married man."

"We heard from a neighbor that his wife paid the bills," Piper told her.

"He claimed the wife was keeping him on a tight leash but..." She shrugged. "He seemed scared."

"Of what?" Piper asked.

"I don't know. Some men don't talk all that much." She shot Piper a sharp look. "Is Leroy in trouble?"

"Two men accused me of taking bribes," Piper said. "One of them just died in a car accident two nights ago."

Venus thrummed her long nails on the table. "Honey, you don't look like the type who goes out for revenge. You aren't threatening Leroy, are you?"

"On the contrary. I want Leroy somewhere safe. I'd love to talk with him."

"But—"

"I said it was an accident—but the police are still investigating. In the meantime, Leroy is now the only person who knows I'm innocent. I don't want anything to happen to him—if you get my drift."

Jack offered Venus a card with the printed number of his cell phone. "If you think of anything else or hear from Leroy, could you give us a call?"

Venus stuffed the card in her bra. "Sure. Be happy to."

But she didn't look happy at all.

After they left, Jack picked up the phone and made a call to his home office. He gave Venus's phone number to the message taker. "I want every word she speaks on her phone, including her cell, for the next forty-eight hours."

Piper looked at him and sighed. "In the last two days since I've been with you I've broken more laws than I have in my entire life."

He winked at her. "You ain't seen nothing yet."

"Promises, promises."

Jack suddenly pulled her close and spoke softly in her ear. "Don't turn around now, but Leroy's peering out of Venus's second-story window at us."

Chapter Eight

Since Jack didn't want Leroy to know that they knew he was there, Piper didn't look up at the window. However, she didn't understand why they were heading away from the house.

She tugged on Jack's shirt. "We should go back and talk to him."

Jack opened the car door and gestured for her to slide in. "He isn't going to tell us anything—"

"You don't know that."

"—or he wouldn't be hiding upstairs."

After she sat in the passenger seat, Jack shut her door with a firm click and walked around the car. Jack had a point, but she didn't want to leave. After all these weeks, she wanted to face her accuser. She wanted to stare the man in the eye and ask him why he'd lied about her. Perhaps she was too emotional to think with Jack's coolheaded logic, yet she felt as though they'd just given up.

"We have nothing to lose by trying."

"Sure we do." Jack started the car and drove out

of the driveway. "If we confront him, he might bolt. And now that we know where he is, we can return any time we want."

"But we might convince him to talk, if we tell him what happened to Vince."

"Don't you think Venus will tell him? And I gave her my cell phone number."

"I guess."

She supposed she was too accustomed to hauling a suspect into police custody and asking questions to readily accept Jack's plan. She'd been good at her job, and her skills at interviewing suspects had become proficient enough that they'd often confessed. But without the power of her badge behind her, wringing a confession out of a guilty party was less iikely. And Jack was right—Venus would tell Leroy about Vince's supposed accident.

"I'm having a hard time staying unemotional about this case," she admitted.

"I know." Jack donned his sunglasses. "But don't be so hard on yourself. Those kinds of reactions are only natural when it's personal."

Did he have to be so understanding? She wanted a good argument right now. To let off a little steam. To steady her nerves. But as usual, he had to go and be difficult—by trying to soothe her, of all things.

She glared at him. "Do women often turn to you for emotional support during your missions?" She wished she could see Jack's eyes. Instead she had to settle for the slight tightening of his neck and jaw muscles.

"My missions don't often bring me into close contact with women." His voice, curt, yet polite, told her as much as the tensed muscles in his forearms that he didn't like the subject matter.

"I wouldn't exactly call this *close* contact, either, would you?" she needled him, watching his fingers clench the steering wheel. When he didn't answer, she poked just a little harder. "What do you have against us being close, Jack?"

He pressed his foot down on the gas pedal. "Are you deliberately trying to distract me?"

"Yes." She leaned over to look at the speedometer and let her breast brush against his arm. A tingle shot through her, warming her all the way from her nipple to between her thighs. Jack's arm flinched. She kept her tone light and playful. "And you're speeding again, Jack."

"Piper."

"Yes?"

"You're nagging. If I wasn't driving, I'd shut you up with a kiss."

A kiss? She was getting to him. So she kept at it. "Nagging you is so much fun. And I haven't had much fun recently." She grinned. "You don't want to deny me a little fun, do you?"

"When your fun is at my expense, I do." He practically growled. "I'm not made of steel."

"Good. Steel doesn't give, and I want you to give in to me, Jack."

"You want total surrender?"

"That wouldn't be so bad, would it?"

As he swallowed hard, she watched his Adam's apple bob in his throat. And was that a bead of sweat glistening on his upper lip?

She sat back in satisfaction at a job well begun. Jack might be pretending right now, but she knew he wasn't a patient kind of man when it came to sexual favors being offered. She could tell by the rasp in his throat and the tension in his shoulders that he now wanted her almost as much as she wanted him. Sooner or later, preferably sooner, he would yield to desire.

And she would get what she wanted. His arms around her. His lips on hers. Just the two of them together flesh to flesh. And she would show him how good they would be together. She already knew they got along well. The spark between them just needed a little kindling to burst into flames.

When Jack turned in to the parking lot of Hodges Computer Systems, she reapplied her lipstick, slicked back a stray hair and faced Jack with an equanimity that surprised her. She hadn't played these kinds of games before, and yet, with Jack she seemed to know exactly what to do. She wasn't holding back. For once, she knew what to say. She knew exactly what she was doing. And it felt good to go after what she wanted.

Every time she knocked Jack off balance, she could feel her feminine powers growing and strengthening.

She might be a late starter. She'd always assumed this kind of flirting wasn't in her. But she'd been wrong. She'd been missing a required element to bring out her natural female tendencies; she'd been missing the right man.

And for her, Jack was the right man. She liked almost everything about him, from the way he protected her, even against himself, to the way he smelled—earthy, yet clean. And she felt comfortable with him, whether hiding in danger behind a desk in a strange house or simply sitting beside him in the car in silence. Oh, yeah. He was definitely the right guy for her. Now all she had to do was convince him. And as much as she wanted to quickly clear her name and win back her job on the police force, she wasn't ready for their investigation to end before she and Jack had more time together.

She was glad that her father had quite a few students that she and Jack would have to interview. Together.

Hodges Computer Systems sold more than just computers. The store had software, printers, scanners and peripherals as well as a repair and technical department. Rock-and-roll music blasted through a state-of-the-art stereo system. Youthful shoppers tested the demo models and helpful salespeople touted the newest technical marvels.

"Aaron Hodges seems to have made quite a success of himself," Piper commented. And somehow the success story didn't fit her mental picture of a man who would plant a virus in the university computer system, burn down her father's house to cover the evidence and then frame her because she was looking into the arson. While she'd met Aaron before—she'd interviewed at least fifty of her father's former students—the man hadn't left much of an impression except that he'd badly wanted to sell her a computer—one he'd constructed out of specialized parts. After she'd told him that she didn't need to upgrade, he'd lost all interest in answering her questions about the fire that had destroyed her parents' home.

Maybe Jack would get more out of him. She put her arm around Jack's waist and leaned in close. "If you pretend you're interested in buying a computer system, Aaron will probably be much more eager to talk to you."

"Understood." Jack put his mouth close to her ear. "I'm going to try and find out if he knows much about hacking."

His lips were close enough to fan his warm breath down her neck. She tucked her arm through his and enjoyed his hard length pressed to hers, and they entered Aaron's office side by side.

Aaron had a large office on the second story of the back of the store. Mirrored windows allowed him to gaze down at his domain without any of his employees knowing whether or not they were being watched. On his walls were pictures of him fishing, pictures of him hunting, pictures of him golfing. A picture of him in military fatigues. In all of them he was alone.

Aaron might not have left much of an impression

on her, but the reverse was not true. Jack had given his name to the secretary to gain entrance into Aaron's office. But when Aaron saw Piper, not only did he recognize her, but his eyes narrowed and he frowned.

He was about an inch shorter than her five foot six, and although he was young to own such a prosperous business, nature had not been kind. He might have a genius IQ, but his mousy brown hair was already thinning. He left the top longer on one side to comb over the bare spots in a ridiculous attempt to hide the obvious. In addition, he wore eyeglasses that slipped down his nose. Yet, in contrast, he'd donned an immaculate suit, shirt and tie, although he worked in an industry known for casual attire.

Aaron didn't even make a pretense at cordiality. He stood up behind his desk and glared at Piper. "What are you doing here?"

"She's with me," Jack said. He stuck out his hand to shake.

Aaron ignored him and spoke to her. "I heard you got fired."

Jack planted both palms on Aaron's desk and loomed over the shorter man. "She brought me here because she said you could hook me up with a fast connection at a reasonable price." He shrugged. "But if you can't…we can go elsewhere."

Aaron wasn't going for Jack's bait. "I sell hardware and software, not connections. Now, if you'll excuse me, I'm a busy man."

Piper figured the guy probably wouldn't be so

openly hostile if he had something to hide. But then again, they weren't looking for the average criminal, either. Aaron had a Ph.D. in computer science. Her father said he was brilliant. Aaron might realize that most people would attempt to look innocent by playing nice, so maybe he'd done the opposite just to try to throw them off.

She didn't like the look of his eyes. Cold. Malevolent. She had to force her feet to remain still and not automatically step closer to Jack.

"Wow!" Jack glanced at the computer, trying a new angle. The computer case he was eyeing featured a window into the computer's heart, and neon lighting showed off circuitry. "You've got an awesome system. What's your ping time?" He reached over and started typing on Aaron's keyboard.

Aaron leaned down and pressed a button, turning off the power to his system. "I suggest you leave before I call a *real* cop."

"Well, you could do that." Jack hitched a hip on Aaron's desk, clearly irritating the entrepreneur. "But we were hoping you might help us out."

"I don't think so."

"Surely you must know something about a computer virus that a student planted in the university computer system back when you attended?" Jack coaxed.

"Why would I?"

"Because if you didn't do it, you probably know who did."

Aaron didn't deny Jack's accusation. "That was a long time ago."

"Something wrong with your memory, dude?" Jack said with just a touch of insult in his tone.

"I might have known a couple of people capable of pulling off that kind of prank. So what?"

"Well, we think that prankster might have committed arson to cover up their crime."

"There's been a fire at the university?" Aaron looked puzzled, but a little too pleased with himself. If she'd had him in a police interview room, she would have left to allow her partner to play bad guy and issue a few threats. However, Jack seemed capable of more than holding his own.

She'd never seen him so intense. He looked like an angry cat, muscles bunched and ready to pounce. And his eyes were such a cool blue that his stare made Aaron shiver.

"No fire at the university." Jack spoke calmly but with an edge of granite in his tone. "Just flames at your old professor's house—but then you knew that, didn't you?"

"That's old news. Of course I knew about the fire. She came here asking me questions about it once before. And I told her I didn't know anything about it. I still don't."

"But you didn't tell her what you knew, did you? Hampering an investigation can be considered a crime."

Jack was good. He threatened by using innocent words.

Aaron's face turned white. "She told me her visit was *unofficial*. And I read in the paper that she was fired—so I'm assuming this investigation is just as unofficial."

"No doubt the arsonist feels safe, since the fire was a while back. Before you built this business. Before you had so much to lose."

"Just what the hell are you insinuating?" Aaron shouted, but Piper could smell the fear in him. And his eyes jerked back and forth from her to Jack as if unsure who presented the greater danger.

"I'm guessing you had the skill to send that virus."

"Lots of us did."

Aaron didn't deny he had the skill. A smart move? They would have known if he'd lied and he knew they would know. Most of the criminals she'd dealt with didn't have half his brains—which made him twice as dangerous.

"Lots?" Jack prodded.

"Okay, maybe a handful." Aaron's face broke into a sweat. He removed a handkerchief from his pocket and swabbed at his forehead.

Jack's voice became conversational. "How about a few names?"

She marveled at his skill. He could turn his voice from friendly to threatening to casual and back in the blink of an eye. And each mood change could throw

Aaron off, possibly cause him to make a mistake and reveal more than he intended.

Aaron loosened his tie. "I don't rat out friends."

"So now the hacker was a friend of yours?" Jack pressed.

"Hey, man. I didn't say that."

"Sure you did. You said you knew who had the skill to do it and that you didn't rat out friends." Jack folded his arms across his chest. "That could make you an accessory to the crime. Did you help with the arson, too?"

"No." Sweat made the glasses slip farther down Aaron's nose. "I did no such thing. Now, get out. And don't come back. You have anything else to say to me, you talk to my attorney. Understand?"

Jack's voice sank to a dangerous whisper that sent a chill down her spine. "I understand why you are afraid."

"Yeah, right." Aaron tried to play tough, but he looked like a rat running for cover.

"Because we're not going to stop until we learn exactly why you are afraid," Jack promised. He slapped his palm on the desk and stood.

Aaron flinched and jerked his thumb at the door. "Get out."

"We're going." Jack's tone was silky smooth. And then he grinned—like a wolf. "But we'll be back."

And then Jack took Piper's arm and they calmly strode from the office. She held back a nervous chuckle by holding her breath and didn't release the air until they'd reached the parking lot. "Jack, you missed your calling."

"I did?"

"Yeah. You play a great good-guy/bad-guy combo all by your lonesome. That was impressive."

"Thanks."

She cast a glance at him. "But now that I've spent more time with you getting to know you better, I've realized that your interviewing skill is not the only thing about you that's impressive."

"You don't stop, do you?"

She slid her hand down his chest to let her fingers toy lightly at his waistband. "Stop? Not a chance. Not until I get what I want."

JACK GRITTED HIS TEETH and tried to ignore the seam of his jeans pressing into his erection. The physical discomfort, as bad as it was, couldn't compare to the psychological wounds she was inflicting. For him, sex had always been easy and plentiful and nothing to get himself into a lather over. But Piper seemed determined to create a new record of how many times she could arouse him in one day. She'd raised being a pest to a new level. And at the same time that she was challenging him to make love, she was raising protective instincts that cut him off at the knees.

He ought to just do it and be done. With any other woman, he would have found the nearest motel and worked her out of his system. They'd both have a good time, burn up the lust over a three-day sexfest, say a friendly goodbye…and never see one another again.

But he couldn't behave that way with Piper. Not when he'd known her all his life. First and foremost, no matter how much she teased and taunted him, he knew she wasn't the kind of woman to have a fling and not look back.

But damn, she looked so fine with her innocent eyes and her sassy mouth that he really, really longed to taste. He had a yen to give her a measure of his lust right this minute, just pull to the side of the road and ravage her mouth, except he wasn't sure he would be able to stop. He couldn't recall the last time he'd wanted to kiss a woman so badly. No doubt about it— she had his guts tied up in knots. And he didn't dare cut loose. Not with Piper—because she had no idea what she was toying with. No idea that the simmering innuendos she kept making were nowhere near as hot and explosive as the ones in his head.

He'd turned up the stereo's volume so that he couldn't hear her teasing. But he could smell her fresh clean hair, the minty aroma of her breath and just a hint of vanilla from either soap or a light perfume.

Keep your eyes on the road.

He refused to look at her cascade of long auburn hair with shimmering golden highlights or her deep-green eyes twinkling with amusement.

As if knowing of his determination not to look at her, she licked her bottom lip, then smoothed the deep-pink gloss with the tip of her pinkie. Damn, he wanted—

Don't look at her.

She fingered the top button of her blouse, unbuttoned it. Then she pulled her shirt from her skin as if she was way too warm. And the loose material allowed him to see the shadow between her breasts, the slight curve where her lacy bra cupped her, and he swallowed hard.

Don't look.

''There.'' She raised her arm and pointed to a two-story brick building with the sign American Breast Cancer Society.

Jack parked the car, but he had a problem. His jeans were so tight that walking was going to be painful. He had no idea if Piper guessed his difficulty, but she grabbed her purse, opened the door and stepped out while he sat behind the wheel, gritting his teeth.

''Would you mind if I go on ahead and use the rest room? I'll meet you in the lobby, okay?''

''Sure.'' Jack slowly released his seat belt and let out the air he'd been holding. This state of affairs couldn't go on for much longer.

After she left, he reviewed his interview with Aaron. And one thing bothered him. Aaron hadn't tried to sell him a system. According to both Piper and her father, Aaron never lost an opportunity to make a sale. But he hadn't even tried. And he'd been damned nervous about Jack seeing his equipment. You could tell a lot about a man from his gear. And Aaron had a custom-built little box from Alienware, a hot CPU and video card, lots of fans to remove heat, a silver case with unique logo, a twenty-two-inch NEC monitor, high-end Audigy sound card from Creative Labs and Klipsch ProMedia 5.1 speakers. Not too shabby.

The dude had bucks and technical knowledge. The picture on the wall of him wearing military fatigues could mean he might have access to mercenary soldiers who for a fee would kill civilians like Vince Edwards. And Aaron disliked cops. But that didn't make him a criminal. They needed to find out what else he might be hiding.

Ten minutes later Jack had himself back under control and met Piper in the lobby. She'd freshened her makeup and done something to her hair, sweeping it up off her neck. But tendrils escaped and twisted and curled in the humidity, softening the look. He wanted to explore the graceful lines of her neck with his lips.

Don't go there.

Danna Mudd wasn't the nerd Piper's father had led them to believe she was. Tall and slender, she wore a navy suit that emphasized the long lean lines of her toned body. Her black hair was styled in a wispy cut that flattered her long face and straight nose. She looked up from her typing the moment they entered her office, but her fingers never stopped flying across the keys.

"Come in, please. Have a seat and I'll just be a moment."

Her office was neat, yet warm with personal touches

like a picture of her with her arms around a man, and a coffee mug decorated with a pink elephant, its nose curled around a string holding balloons.

Danna hit the save key, then looked at them with a friendly smile. "Sorry, I had to finish the thought before I lost it. What can I do for you folks?"

Her friendly attitude, so in contrast to that of Aaron Hodges, wouldn't deter Jack from asking his questions, but he took his cue from the suspect and responded in kind. "I'm Jack Donovan, and this is Piper Payne."

"We once spoke briefly over the phone, right?" Without hesitation Danna shook their hands.

"You probably remember Piper's father, too." Jack wanted to pace instead of sitting beside Piper on the love seat, but he didn't want Danna to feel as though she was being attacked. So he sat, trying not to let any part of his body come into contact with any part of Piper's.

"Professor Payne taught one of my computer science classes at the university." Danna's expression was one of fondness. "He was one of my favorite teachers. In fact, I had a crush on him for a short time."

At Piper's raised eyebrows, Danna chuckled. "Oh, nothing ever came of my infatuation. Professor Payne would have been horrified if he'd known I fantasized about him. Well, that's probably way more than you wanted to know, but I assure you he never had a clue—and I was much too naive to even speak up in class, never mind in any kind of personal way.''

Jack filed the information away. Danna might be telling the truth. Or she might have had a sizzling-hot affair with Professor Payne and figured that admitting to a crush might sweep away any deeper suspicions. Still, knowing Piper's dad, Jack couldn't picture the man cheating on his wife.

''We were hoping you might help us,'' Piper said. ''Do you recall a computer virus a few years ago that shut down the university's systems for a day or two?''

''Vaguely. Why?''

''Well, my dad was in charge of investigating the virus. And he kept information about his search at home. Last year an arsonist burned Dad and Mom's house to the ground.''

''I'm so sorry.'' Danna frowned. ''You think whoever started the fire might have done it to burn up the evidence your father collected about the virus?''

''It's just a theory,'' Piper admitted. She didn't go into how she'd been framed and lost her job on the police force. ''I'm trying to talk to Dad's old students to see if any of them knew who had written the virus.''

Danna shook her head. ''I was never into hacking. I think that's a challenge that appeals more to the male gender.''

''Can you remember any students who were into that kind of thing?'' Jack asked.

''Well, let me think.'' Danna closed her eyes, then opened them and stared at Jack. ''There's Aaron

Hodges. He used to brag about how he could get into the Defense Department, although I doubt it was true.''

''Why?'' Piper asked.

Danna shrugged. ''Just a feeling. He seemed all talk and no action, but I could be wrong.''

''Can you think of anyone else?'' Jack prodded.

''Well, there was Easy As Pie. I never knew his real name, but the guy was quite a character. And let me tell you, he gave me the willies. Always wore black. Black shirt, black pants and black trench coat. And he was secretive. Wouldn't look me in the eye.''

''Have you any idea where we might find him?''

''Nope.'' Danna grinned. ''But I can give you a lead. A few months ago I went bowling with the girls over at Clearwater Lanes. And I saw the guy on the end two alleys. He had one of those custom balls, all black sparkles.''

''Did you talk to him?'' Jack asked.

''No. He still wears black, and he had a military tattoo on his arm.''

''You recognized the tattoo?'' Jack asked.

''My brother was in the military.'' A fleeting look of pain crossed her face. ''Anyway, when I returned my rental shoes, I mentioned Easy As Pie to the clerk, who said he's there all the time. Never talks to anyone. Creepy.''

''Thanks.'' Jack appreciated Danna's help; however, he wondered if she'd been just a little too helpful, especially just happening to mention the military tattoo. He suspected that she might know much more than she was saying.

Jack and Piper left the building. "Let's head over to Clearwater Lanes and talk to the shoe clerk. Maybe he'll remember more."

"Okay." Piper batted her eyelashes at him and he steeled himself for another of her blatant come-ons. Sure enough, she didn't disappoint him. "But bowling wasn't exactly the kind of recreational activity I had on my mind."

LEROY HAD his instructions. And he'd better follow them like a good little soldier. Time was running out for taking care of this little problem and closing the deal.

The Cayman bank account was set to go. The information was ready and the buyer was salivating to make the purchase. But the buyer was cagey, watching, not willing to take any chances.

Today the bait was set. Payne and Donovan couldn't help but nibble. And one nibble would be all it took to finish them off.

The Shey Group and the police department might suspect foul play, but by the time they put the pieces together, their suspect would be long gone. Living the good life on the French Riviera. Or maybe in Rio. Ah, yes. A hot beach, lots of sunshine. And no more nightmares over a stubborn female cop and her mysterious boyfriend.

This plan was practically foolproof. Because surely today they would die.

Chapter Nine

"We've picked up a tail." Jack had spotted the green sedan almost immediately after leaving the American Breast Cancer Society. But he'd waited a few minutes to be sure of the driver's identity before speaking.

Piper sighed. "Jack, if you want me to take my clothes off again, you don't have to pretend that I've picked up another bug."

He supposed her assumption was his fault. He'd spoken in a conversational tone. And apparently she'd picked up on his laid-back attitude and had followed that to her own conclusions.

"Look in your mirror at the green sedan. That's Leroy following us."

"Green? I wonder if his paint might match the scrape marks on Vince's car?" Piper sat up straighter to check the mirror. "Maybe we should stop and have a conversation."

"There are lots of green cars on the road." Jack knew she was itching to face the man who'd accused her of bribery. In her position he'd probably have felt the same way. However, he had to consider all the angles. "It's odd that he didn't follow us after we left Venus, but picked us up since our talk with Danna."

Piper peered at Jack over the rim of her sunglasses. "Maybe he followed us from Venus's house, and you missed him."

"You have a way of distracting me, Pest—"

"I'm not a pest."

"But I'd have to be comatose—"

"That could be arranged."

"—to miss a tail as inept as he is."

Piper scowled at him. "Okay, okay. If you think I'm going to believe that I'm not woman enough to distract the great tail spotter—"

"You do have a nice one," he commented, figuring to give her a little payback.

"Nice what?"

"A nice tail. Firm. Shapely. The kind a man likes to wrap his hands around."

"Jack, don't you dare put suggestions in my head that you don't intend to follow through on." She might be complaining, but he saw the corner of her mouth quirk up at his compliment. In fact, she looked way too pleased with herself. No doubt because he was heating up all over again.

She pressed the sunglasses back onto the bridge of her nose. "If you don't want to talk to Leroy, are you going to lose him?"

"Not yet. Let's see what he does next."

She fluffed her hair, using that as an excuse to check

the mirror again. "How did he pick us up at Danna's office? We didn't mention our next destination to Venus, did we?"

"Not that I can recall. But maybe someone was expecting us to talk to Danna."

"Who?"

"The same person who talked Vince and Leroy into claiming you took a bribe."

"I don't know. You're really reaching here."

"Not necessarily. Your father's former students all knew one another—we just don't know how well. And we didn't hide our intentions from any of them about talking to the others."

She rubbed her forehead. "That would mean Aaron or Danna is the one we're looking for."

"Not necessarily."

"Now you're making even bigger assumptions."

"Yeah, but suppose Aaron or Danna knows Easy As Pie—not too unlikely, since they went to school together. Suppose Aaron or Danna called and warned Easy about us?"

"So then Easy calls Leroy at his mistress's house and tells him to follow us?" She shook her head. "And you're sure Leroy found us *after* we left Danna."

He didn't bother responding to her insult. "Maybe someone guessed who we would interview next."

"Yeah. And maybe we have another bug on this car. You sure you don't want to take off your clothes?" she teased.

"Don't start. I'm not in the mood."

"What are you in the mood for, Jack?"

There she went again, putting into his head damning images of the two of them together. She really had no sense of honor. Didn't she know what those words could do to a man? All his blood was aiming south again.

Think of something else.

Piper crossed one leg over the other. She let her sandal dangle from her toes as she rocked her foot up and down. Suggestively. She was lucky he didn't just pull over to the curb and make love to her on the car's trunk.

"What's wrong?" she asked him. "You have this almost pained look on your face."

"Nothing's wrong," he snapped.

She shifted in her seat and checked her lipstick in the mirror. "Leroy's still there."

If she had any idea what the pad of her pinkie smoothing her lip gloss was doing to him, she wouldn't have been as concerned about the man following her—as she was about the man next to her. After all, he was no saint. He could take only so much.

"Will you sit still?" he practically growled.

She started playing with her top shirt button. "No need to get testy."

This couldn't go on. As the pressure increased in his jeans, he sorted through strategies. If he admitted his discomfort, she was more likely to intensify her efforts to seduce him rather than abandon them.

Still without a solution, he drove into the bowling alley's parking lot. ''Maybe I should let you talk to the shoe clerk.''

She peered at him with a perplexed expression. ''Why? Aren't you up for it?''

He was *up,* all right. Sometimes male anatomy could be a huge disadvantage. Women could so easily hide their arousal and keep a man guessing. Yet here he was front and center with an erection as hard as the Washington Monument and nowhere to hide.

He rolled his eyes at the car's ceiling. ''I figured you could nag the information out of the guy better than I could.''

''Fine. Watch my back.''

He'd watch her back and the enticing sway of her hips. He'd watch those long legs of hers cross the hot pavement. And he'd give himself time to recover.

She finally got out of the car, glanced toward where Leroy had parked and spoke through the still-open door. ''Anything in particular that you want me to go after?''

''Easy's address.''

When she came back several minutes later with a huge smile on her face, he knew she'd been successful. She slid into the cool air-conditioning and snapped on her seat belt. ''It's much easier to get teenage boys to talk when I'm not wearing a business suit.''

No kidding. She could probably entice a lion to surrender his dinner. He kept the thought to himself, pleased that his lower half was once again cooperating. "Where to?"

She gave him the address, and he gunned the engine to wake up Leroy. Jack didn't want the man to fall asleep and lose them. Because he did intend to question the man, but just not yet. Sometimes waiting could prey on a man's mind. Jack figured Leroy was running scared after learning about Vince's accident. Time could increase Leroy's anxiety, and then he might be more ready to talk.

Piper checked her watch and dug in her purse for the cell phone Logan Kincaid had supplied. "Time to call the department. The shift changed at three."

Three? They'd skipped lunch and his stomach hadn't even growled. Funny how time passed so quickly when Piper was around. With all of her badgering, she kept him hungry for more than lunch.

"Hey, Calvin." She spoke in a congenial tone that she rarely used with him. "Got any news for me?"

She'd hit the speaker button so Jack could listen. The police investigator, Cal, spoke with a thick Southern drawl. "This was no accident."

"You're sure?"

"The brake line was slashed clean and even the parking brake was disengaged."

So Vince had been murdered. By whom? And was it simply a coincidence that Vince had accused her of bribery? Lots of people might have wanted the man dead.

"Any luck on the green paint from the other car?"

"Not yet. Forensics is behind schedule. The chief put priority on a double homicide. So it's going to be a while, maybe another day or two."

"Thanks, Cal. I appreciate the info."

"Sure. How about dinner next week?"

She didn't glance Jack's way, but he still did his best to remain stoic. With a face, body and personality like hers, he imagined guys hit on her all the time. Still, he didn't need to know.

"The week after might be better."

"I'll give you a call, okay?"

"Sure."

Jack noticed that Cal didn't ask for her phone number. Probably because he knew it by heart. Maybe slept with it under his pillow and dreamed of her every night. He couldn't blame the guy, and yet he didn't much like it, either.

With other women, Jack never gave their social life a thought. If they weren't with him, then they weren't with him. Their loss, and end of story. He shouldn't care what Piper did or whom she saw when he wasn't around, and yet…he did care. Which irritated him, because they hadn't even made love. Hell, they weren't even really friends.

She hung up the phone and waited a few minutes before speaking. "You're awfully quiet."

"Hmm."

"Cal and I are friends."

"I didn't ask."

"Yeah, but your silence speaks volumes."

"So now you can read my mind?"

"It's not that difficult."

He frowned. "Are you saying I'm simple?"

"I'm saying that you are *male*. And men think about sex 24/7. So it's only natural that you're wondering about Cal and me." She patted Jack's thigh, and he bit back a growl. "It's okay, Jack. On the police force I worked around a lot of men. Long enough to know that the males of the species can't help themselves when it comes to speculating about women."

Jack had had enough of her condescending pats on his thigh. He'd had enough of her teasing. It was her fault he thought about sex 24/7. She kept touching him and riding him. What red-blooded male wouldn't be in need of sexual release right about now?

He brought the car to a screeching halt on the side of the road. He unfastened his seat belt, got out and slammed the door.

She was two steps behind him, seemingly mystified by his erratic behavior. The concern in her face irritated him all the more. Next she'd be offering to kiss him and make him all better.

"What's wrong?"

"Maybe you should read my mind."

"Come on, Jack."

"Well, I was thinking about the case," he lied, just to bug her. "And I think it's time we talked to Leroy and reminded him that Vince didn't die in an accident."

"Fine."

He started walking toward Leroy, who had pulled over across the street next to a sandwich shop. Piper grabbed Jack's hand and pulled him to a stop on the sidewalk.

"I'm sorry, Jack." She looked up into his eyes and then wrapped her arms around him to give him a hug. And of course his body leaped to attention again.

He didn't stop to think.

He didn't say a word. He just dipped his head and kissed her. He didn't bother with slow and easy. He kissed her demandingly, taking what he wanted, holding her close enough to lose track of where he ended and she began. Close enough to feel her heart rate skyrocket. Close enough to feel her arms winding around his neck and pulling him against her.

Piper kissed him as if there would be no tomorrow. She put everything into her kiss, holding back nothing. And he took her sweetness and her passion and then demanded more, encouraging her with his lips and tongue.

And with their bodies pressed together, she had to know the effect she was having on him. Finally he regained a measure of sanity and pulled back. His breath ragged, he watched her eyes flutter open as she released him reluctantly. Her pupils were glazed with passion, her lips swollen from his kiss.

But most of all, she looked happy. Happy to be standing on a sidewalk and kissing him in broad daylight as if they might not live another minute. As if there would be no consequences from the kiss.

But with a woman like Piper there would always be consequences. He shouldn't have kissed her, but Jack wasn't one for should haves and could haves. He dealt with reality. And the facts clearly stated that when they came together, they set off a spontaneous combustion. Even now, from two feet away, her heat seared his senses.

She raised her hand and touched her fingers to her lips. "Wow."

Yeah, wow. He hoped to hell she couldn't read the guilt he was feeling right now. She'd be angry that he felt responsible for her. He didn't want to hurt her, but he surely would when he wrapped up this case, ended his vacation and walked away. Another man might have stayed. But Jack wasn't good enough for her. She deserved someone better than him. Someone stable, maybe someone like her friend Cal.

The thought annoyed the hell out of him, but he respected her enough to walk away before he did real damage. He took her hand and tugged her toward Leroy. "Come on, sugar."

"Don't call me sugar."

"Why not? You sure are one sweet—"

She dug her elbow into his side.

"Ow."

"It won't work, Jack."

"What?"

"You can't kiss me like that and then try to push me away with chauvinistic insults. I won't let you do that."

Damn her. She'd seen right through him. How the hell had she gotten so smart? And if she was so smart, why didn't she have the sense to stay away from him?

When he'd kissed her, she could have stopped him by stomping on his foot. Or kicking his shins. But she hadn't fought him. *Oh, no.* She'd drawn him closer and kissed him with a brave heat that had burned and branded.

"Come on, Jack." She tugged him toward the street. "We can finish what's between us later. I want to talk to Leroy."

"There's nothing to finish."

"Oh, really?" She glanced at his crotch. "Your body says different."

A car honked, saving him from an answer. She really was the most irritating woman he'd ever met. She'd just kissed him as if she was on fire and then had coolly put her feelings aside and announced that she wanted to question Leroy. Sheesh. And he thought women were supposed to be the emotional sex. With the crazy way she had him feeling right now, he sure was glad they weren't in danger, because he was having trouble breathing, never mind focusing.

Crossing the busy road proved more difficult than Jack had expected. Across the street Leroy seemed resigned to waiting for them. He even waved for them to join him while he spoke into his cell phone.

The four-lane highway didn't have a median strip, and they waited a good four minutes before the traffic lightened enough for them to begin a mad dash across the street. Jack was holding Piper's hand.

Out of the corner of his eye he caught a flash of light. A pressure change registered in his eardrums.

Bomb.

Instantly he reacted, yanking Piper to the pavement and falling on top of her.

"Are you craz—"

A deafening boom cut off her words. Heat and flames shattered the glass in Leroy's car. And the glass in the sandwich shop next to his car.

Fire enveloped the car, along with the man standing next to the blazing vehicle. At the blast of hot air, Jack held his breath and tried to protect Piper from the burning pieces of metal raining down on them like confetti.

Piper struggled against him, but he held her down, assuming the motorists would halt before they ran over them as they lay in.the middle of the road.

When the metal stopped falling, Jack sat up and peered at her through black smoke. "You okay?"

"I will be just fine once you stop crushing me into the pavement."

He stood and helped Piper to her feet. Her face was blackened with soot. Their new clothes were ruined by the oil from the pavement, the soot and the smoke. She paid no attention to her appearance—not the blood trickling from the cut on her chin, not the bruise darkening on her shoulder where she'd fallen—but stepped toward the burning car. "Leroy?"

He blocked her from heading in that direction. "There's nothing you can do."

Jack didn't have to look more closely to know the man hadn't survived. Leroy had been standing at ground zero. That bomb had gone off from inside his car, probably from under the driver's seat, and he'd been standing right next to the vehicle.

Jack had seen death before. Too many times. It always saddened him. But this time frustration entered the mix.

Jack had screwed up. Big time.

Piper had wanted to face her accuser. Talk to Leroy sooner. He'd insisted she wait for the right moment, and now she'd lost her chance. Forever.

And now both of the citizens who'd gotten her fired were dead.

If Jack hadn't spent every moment with Piper, if he hadn't known her as he did, he might have thought *she* had taken revenge on the people who had wronged her. He might have thought she had arranged their deaths. And Jack feared the police might come to just that conclusion.

Piper was still edging toward the flames. But the heat was so intense that she couldn't make any progress.

Jack tugged her back. "We need to get out of here."

She frowned at him as if he'd lost his mind. "We need to stay until the bomb squad—"

"Whoever set off that bomb might try again."

"But we weren't the target. Leroy was."

"We were mere footsteps from meeting him. If we hadn't paused and kissed, we might all be dead. That's a coincidence I can't ignore. And whoever set off the bomb might be in this crowd. The next time, they might get us. We have to leave now."

"You really think that we were the target?"

"Yeah. Let's get out of here." He tugged her harder, giving her no choice but to go with him. A crowd of onlookers had gathered, but Jack shouldered between the bystanders until they reached their car. "Get in."

She didn't argue.

Jack heard police and ambulance sirens heading their way. He slid behind the wheel, made a U-turn and headed in the opposite direction. At the first corner he made a hard right and watched the rearview mirror. No one appeared to follow, but that didn't ease his nerves.

He should have been more careful. After the fire at Leroy's home, after they'd ditched the bug, he'd known they were up against a dangerous adversary. Somehow he'd ignored the very real possibility that someone wanted Piper dead.

His mental lapse could have gotten her killed.

And he knew exactly what was wrong with him. He'd been thinking about how good she smelled and how fine she looked. He could have kicked himself when he recalled how he'd been kissing her on the sidewalk in broad daylight only moments before the explosion. Never before had he been so irresponsible. Which only went to prove how far gone he was over her.

"Jack, you stopped the car without planning to. How could anyone have known that we would be approaching Leroy at that second?"

"They didn't have to know *when.* They only had to know that we *would* talk to him. So they watched and waited for Leroy to meet with us and that's when they made their move."

"How could they know?"

"The person who bugged us knew we went to Leroy's house. It's not hard to figure out we might try to get in touch with him again. So they waited. And picked their moment."

"But how did the bomb go off in the exact instant we were about to meet with Leroy?"

"The bomb's timer was most likely set by a remote control device. Or they could have set off the bomb by a noise on Leroy's phone."

"If they were aiming for us, why didn't they wait until we got closer?"

"Maybe they miscalculated the delay. We're talking maybe another second or two, that's all."

"So whoever set off the bomb was…how far away?"

"Within five hundred yards. Why?"

She plucked her cell phone from her purse and dialed. "Aaron Hodges, please."

Smart woman. While she checked on Hodges's

whereabouts, he phoned Danna Mudd. If either of them were at work, then they couldn't have been close enough to set off the bomb—unless they'd hired help.

She hung up and told him, "Aaron had some errands to run. He wasn't in."

"Neither was Danna. Damn." They were hitting dead ends. One right after the other, and he wouldn't have minded if he could have crossed just one suspect off their list. But now he had to add Venus to the list, since she was one of the people who knew they were looking for Leroy. The stripper had told Leroy about them. She might have sent Leroy to follow them. But if she was involved, he had no idea how. But that had been his problem from the start.

Leroy had no motive for arson or murder. He had no idea why anyone would have gone to such elaborate lengths to frame Piper. But experience told him they weren't up against an ordinary criminal.

Piper's mind had taken a different tack. "I wish I knew who Leroy was speaking to during his phone call."

He must have been shook up but good not to think of that angle himself, Jack thought. "If the phone was registered in his name, the records will be available." He made a quick phone call to the Shey Group's home office and put in his request.

"Where are we going?" Piper asked.

"To John Smith aka Easy As Pie's residence."

"We look like refugees from a war zone. Maybe we should clean up first."

"No."

"Don't I get a say?"

He didn't want to go to a hotel with her. He didn't need more distractions. They needed to concentrate on this case and solve it. He put some urgency into his tone. "We waited too long to talk to Leroy. I don't want to wait and miss—"

"You don't need to feel guilty."

What? Did he have "guilt" written on his forehead? Because if so, he might need to find a new profession.

That she was so good at reading him took him aback. He didn't want to be so transparent. Usually he wasn't. And if he wasn't, then she'd connected with him on levels so scary that he really didn't want to think about them.

His phone rang. "Leroy James—" one of the Shey Group's information specialists had called Jack back "—doesn't have a cell phone registered in his name."

"What about a phone in the name Venus De Lux?"

"Nothing. However, Leroy's wife has a phone, but it was reported stolen last week."

"Has anyone used that number?"

"Let me check and get back to you, okay? By the way, Adam wants you to call him."

Jack dialed Adam's number. "You have something for me?"

"Yeah. Your guy is smart." Adam's voice came in clearly, but sounded faint.

Jack upped the phone's volume. "We're looking for a male?"

"Normally I'd say yes. Females aren't usually into computer hacking, but that makes the ones who are even more dangerous."

"Got it."

"You're probably dealing with someone brilliant and unstable. Probably a sociopath. The world revolves around him and anyone who gets in the way will be squashed. Your guy is ruthless. And a coward."

"Aren't those traits contradictory?" Jack asked.

"When he feels he's in control, he takes pleasure in manipulating. But once he's threatened, he may go underground. Or run."

"Understood."

"The guy's dangerous. Don't underestimate him."

"Vulnerabilities?" Jack asked.

"Once you chase him out of his territory, he might make a stupid mistake. He believes he knows it all and can handle anything. Push him from his comfort zone, and he'll still think he's invincible—that's when you catch him."

"Thanks, Adam."

"Keep sending me information and I might have more for you later."

"Anything else?"

"Like any wild animal, he'll be most dangerous when cornered. I repeat, use extreme caution."

LEROY WAS DEAD and he could roast in hell. Too bad he'd be alone.

The SOB hadn't had the decency to take Payne and

Donovan with him. According to the police scanners, the bombing had killed only one victim. An Afro-American male. The sorry excuse for a man could do nothing right.

Apparently if I want this done right, I will have to do it myself.

Yet killing them wouldn't be easy. Donovan had skills. And Payne was no pushover.

The smart thing would be to hire a professional. But that left loose ends. And associating with criminals was so incredibly disgusting. Those people were little better than animals. They had no class, no intelligence and no idea that there was more to life than drugs, booze and getting laid. And even worse, they couldn't be counted on to remain loyal.

No more relying on idiots. No more mistakes could be allowed. The buyers were silent, hadn't even acknowledged the last e-mail. Moving quickly was essential before the buyers bought the information from another source.

This time there would be no error.

Chapter Ten

Piper had cleaned her face and Jack's with tissue from her purse. However, there was nothing she could do about their sooty clothes. After they questioned Easy, Piper planned to go to a hotel and take a long hot shower. Preferably with Jack.

If his erotic kiss was any indication, he was heating up just as she'd planned. It was a shame that the memory of their first real kiss had to be marred by a man's death.

Although she'd wanted to confront Leroy about his false accusation, although she was angry that he had contributed to a scam that had gotten her fired, she hadn't wanted revenge. At least the explosion had killed him in the initial blast. Quite likely, Leroy hadn't suffered and hadn't had time to realize what had happened. One moment he'd been alive and well, and the next he was gone forever.

And she and Jack could have died with him. Which hadn't changed her priorities, only reinforced them. Now more than ever Piper wanted Jack to be the one to take her virginity. She didn't want to wait any longer. Although she hadn't changed so much that she was now thinking she should live for today and not worry about tomorrow, she didn't want to put her life on hold, waiting for a man and a future that might not happen.

Jack was here. Today. And they shared a chemistry that couldn't be denied.

Tonight, she promised herself. Tonight's the night.

She didn't say a word to Jack about her plans. Instead, she admired the leaded-glass front doors of the ranch-style home and the old-fashioned mail slot manufactured right into the creative design.

"This is another ritzy address," Piper told Jack as they walked up the steps to the front doors. "I wonder what Easy does for a living?"

Jack rang the bell, and chimes announced their presence. Piper almost expected a butler to answer the door. She remembered John Smith's face from a picture, it had been taken during his last year in computer class. The man had fanatical eyes and had worn black in that picture, too, just as her father and Danna had said. According to other students, he'd always been hostile and uncooperative, and she had no reason to think he'd changed.

"What do you want?" A man's voice came through the front door.

She tried to peer through the glass, but between the stained panels and the beveled edges of the clearer sections, she couldn't see anything beyond a dark-clad silhouette. How the guy had ever earned the nickname Easy was beyond her. John Smith, if that was him behind the door, struck her as antisocial and hard-edged. Nothing easy about him.

Jack pounded on the door. "Either you open the door or I'll call the cops."

Huh? What was Jack thinking?

Surprisingly, his threat worked. The man opened the door.

"You John Smith?" Jack asked.

"Yeah." He stood about six foot five and looked like a slab of solid muscle. With his black T-shirt, black jeans and black boots, he could have been a professional football player—even down to his hostile leer. But the burning cigarette dangling from his mouth spoiled the image of a superstar athlete. "So?"

"We want to talk to you about…business." Jack put his arm over Piper's shoulder, and she could have sworn he leered at her—just a little.

She had no idea where Jack was going with his act, but she played along. And snuggled right up against him. For once he didn't pull back. Perhaps their siz-zling kiss had set him straight.

She might have been clueless, but Easy seemed to know what Jack was *not* saying.

"Look, I don't take clients off the street." Easy eyed their sooty clothes suspiciously. "Where'd you get my name?"

Clients? Off the street? He sounded as if he was

into something illegal. Computers. Internet. Illegal. Porn?

Jack's hand had suddenly gotten very friendly with her shoulder. His fingers drifted south toward her breast. And she'd been around him long enough to know that he wasn't making a move on her. No, Jack's calculated touch had to be to create an impression for a reason she had yet to fathom.

She trusted him enough to go along. Very deliberately she placed her hand on his buttock. And squeezed. Then she looked up at him innocently.

Jack's eyes danced with heat. There would be consequences for her actions. Later. Consequences she'd be happy to accept in exchange for the opportunity to tease him now.

"Found you on the Internet," Jack explained.

"My address isn't listed."

"I did a little hacking," Jack admitted.

Jack hadn't hacked the address. She'd gotten it from the shoe rental clerk at the bowling alley, but she supposed it paid for him to cover their tracks. Besides, the admission made Jack appear to be part of the criminal underworld and might cause Easy to relax.

"I wasn't sure I had the correct address until I saw the matching logo from this side of the door. Pretty cool." Jack's admission gave her the clue she needed. He hadn't told her more because he hadn't known until he'd seen the glass doors from this side. Apparently the image matched something he'd seen on the Internet.

Jack's fingers sent delicious shivers down her arm. And as they walked into a black-mirrored and black-tiled foyer that could have used a good dusting, she tilted back her head to look up at the black ceiling and restrained her frown of disapproval. From here she could see living and dining rooms, and every piece of furniture in them was black.

What a nut case.

"Then you know how I work," Easy said to Jack. "Two grand for one hour. Cash. Up front."

Two thousand dollars? For what? Piper didn't ask, but continued to play along.

Jack opened his wallet and peeled off hundred-dollar bills. "You have costumes for the lady?"

Uh-oh. *Costumes?*

"Sure."

"And I'd like a look around."

"We have bedrooms with some interesting decorations. You have a fetish—I've got a room with the right paraphernalia and props. And you'll have a better chance of earning back your investment."

Earning back his investment? Piper tried to keep the confusion from her face. The man was making pornography? Apparently Jack's program had run down her father's students and picked up those with questionable businesses, information that he hadn't shared with her.

Renting a room and charging outrageous prices might not exactly be illegal, but the city commissioners would frown on it. That meant hassles from the press and police. Was that why Easy hadn't wanted to speak with Detective Payne? He hadn't wanted her snooping into his business and scaring away his clients?

"While she's picking out her outfit, could I look at some finished video product online?" Jack asked. "Might give me a few ideas."

Double uh-oh. She swallowed hard. Apparently they were renting a room for kinky sex to be broadcast over the Internet. She wanted her job back, but she would go only so far to get it. And kinky sex on the Internet was definitely crossing over her line.

But she could play along for a while. Obviously Jack wanted in to Easy's system. And while he played with the keyboard, he clearly wanted her to distract Easy by trying on costumes, but for all they knew, he might be bored with women's lingerie by now. Piper wanted to punch the air out of Jack's lungs, but instead she pasted a bright smile on her face.

"I do so adore trying on clothes." She wriggled against Jack. "Darling, this is going to be so much fun." And then with a hand behind Jack's back, a hand Easy couldn't see, she squeezed his butt again, harder this time. Not that she could make a dent in his buns of steel, but taking out her frustration on him gave her more than a bit of satisfaction.

Jack stepped back, but not before swatting her rear in a playful gesture. "Go on and enjoy yourself, babe. You know my taste, don't you?"

She raised an eyebrow. "Why, I didn't know you

had any taste. I thought you just wanted me to show up naked...with beer.''

Over her head Easy and Jack chuckled, but then Jack's eyes locked warmly with hers. ''Naked is fine, but a man always appreciates a good striptease first.''

She filed away that little tidbit for later use. Jack had been kidding, but if that fantasy was the first that had popped into his mind, it must be one he enjoyed. And tonight she wanted both of them to enjoy some private time together.

Business first. She linked her arm through Easy's and did her best to keep the dread out of her tone. ''Let's go, sugar. I'll model a few outfits, and you can give me your opinion.''

Surely his costumes couldn't be worse than a bikini. Or the prostitute's outfit she'd worn on the street during a neighborhood cleanup operation, but then she'd had backup, officers who would come in to help her if she murmured a code word into her hidden microphone. Here she was on her own—except for Jack.

Of course, she trusted Jack. But he couldn't be in two places at once.

After showing Jack his computer system, Easy led her upstairs and into a walk-in closet the size of most people's living rooms. All four walls were lined with shelves and were full of gadgets and costumes, everything from shiny black leather and chains to whips and paddles.

Most of the outfits were see-through, skimpy and barely there. She strode past endless rows of spiked high heels, clear storage drawers filled with stockings and garters. And there was every kind of undergarment ever made in a wide variety of colors and styles. Most of them indecent.

In the hope it would cover her, she took a nurse's uniform off the hanger. But the uniform had clear plastic pull-away Velcro cutouts. No way. Not with Easy's fanatical eyes slicing her up for a gourmet lunch.

Next she took an *I Dream of Jeanie* costume off the rack. Multicolored gauze covered the arms and legs and the material left a bare midriff, but the essentials were covered. However, she could have done without the tassels on the bra.

"This might do." Piper carried the outfit behind a curtained-off changing area. She immediately spied the Webcam, which she blocked with her purse before starting to undress. She didn't want to raise Easy's suspicions by moving too slowly, yet she intended to drag out each costume change for as long as possible. Jack was going to owe her big time for every minute she had to stall.

When she finally exited the cubicle to stand before a three-way mirror, she had to refrain from cringing. In the harem clothing she looked like some kind of love slave. Yet from the way Easy was eyeing her in dissatisfaction, she guessed she wasn't showing enough skin.

Easy frowned. "Since you seem undecided, maybe I'll go help lover boy pick a room. We have one that matches that costume."

"Really?" Although she was willing to go only so far, she had to keep him here. She couldn't let him leave and find Jack hacking into his computer. "Maybe you could help me find something a little more revealing?"

At her words, Easy turned back to her. His eyes glimmered with renewed sleaze, but at least he'd given up on the idea of visiting Jack. He pulled out a camisole with matching panties that were all lace and bows—with no lining. Wearing that offering would be the equivalent of going naked.

She peered at the flimsy material as if trying to decide. "I'm worried about—"

"Germs?" Easy leered at her. "After a session I have everything professionally cleaned. Even the bed linens and towels. I run a first-class operation."

"Okay." She took the teddy and retreated to the dressing room. A few minutes later she came back out—fully dressed. And she could see the disappointment in his eyes.

"Sorry, the panties were too large." *Yeah right.* The only reason she'd even pulled them above her knees, but no farther up, was that he could see her feet and calves below the curtain.

"Ah." Easy reached into the rack and extracted a pale pink bodysuit that was barely there. "Try this one. It stretches. One size fits all."

She nodded her thanks and again retreated to the cubicle. Where the hell was Jack? Piper was beginning to run out of excuses. But she went through the process of removing her slacks, then pulling the material over her knees. Then she waited as if she were really trying on the pink thingy.

She spoke from behind the curtain. "This color is all wrong. My skin looks sallow."

"It also comes in black." Easy tossed her a black outfit.

Great. All the times she'd gone shopping, no man had ever been so helpful. And now she was excuse-challenged. She'd never been much of a shopper. She'd complained about size, style and color. What else was there?

JACK'S FINGERS FLEW over the system. He'd hacked past Easy's fire wall, but had lost precious minutes finding a way past his Internet guard dogs. The defense system, surprisingly sophisticated, had him suspicious. Once he got a crack and worked his way inside, he restrained a whistle. Easy's operation was unbelievably profitable.

He copied Easy's e-mail address book and forwarded it to his system. But a cursory search found no mention of Vince, Leroy, Danna or Aaron.

Time to go.

Carefully he hid his tracks, covered his entry and exit, dismantled the warning bells and whistles, then set them back to default before slipping out of the system. As a matter of course he left a back door open, so if he wanted to return he could now do so from any Internet connection.

He'd rushed, but he'd been thorough. And as he checked his watch, he realized that Piper had been alone with the porn king for longer than he'd intended. Although he knew she could handle herself, Jack took the stairs three at a time.

The minute he entered the costume room, Easy's face gave him a clue that he hadn't arrived a minute too soon. The lines on his face had deepened into dark scowls. And his meaty hands had closed into fists.

"Lady, you are the finickiest—"

"*Finickiest* isn't a word." Piper's voice came from inside a changing booth. Jack could see her bare legs and feet and didn't like the fact that Easy was staring at them as if she was to be his next meal.

Easy had yet to spot Jack. "I don't need any damn English lessons from the likes of you."

"Maybe not. But you could learn some manners."

Easy's face reddened. He puffed up his chest like an angry bull ready to charge.

Jack cleared his throat, then chuckled. "I always call her the Pest."

"Thanks a lot," she muttered, but he thought he'd caught a measure of relief in her tone.

Jack rolled his eyes at the ceiling as Easy turned to look at him. "Once she figures out which buttons to press—"

"And I know all your hot buttons, don't I, sweetheart?" she muttered in the most fake, sugary-sweet tone he'd ever heard, which told him she wasn't just annoyed, but perhaps a little scared, although she'd never admit it.

"That's why I keep her around," Jack told Easy with a man-to-man grin. "She's annoying as hell, but that mouth of hers isn't just sassy…it's talented."

"Did you decide on a room?" Easy's attention now focused on Jack, just as he'd intended. Whatever had been going on before he'd arrived had been temporarily set aside, if not forgotten.

"Which room is the most popular?" Jack asked.

"The waterfall."

"I can't swim," Piper protested.

She could swim like a fish, and *she* knew *he* knew it. Obviously she was telling him that they'd taken their little venture far enough. But he wanted to extract them without creating more suspicion.

"It won't hurt you to take a look at the water, maybe slide in up to your ankles," Jack coaxed.

"I'll go warm up the equipment. That room is downstairs." Easy turned and left the huge closet.

Piper barged out of the dressing room, her face flushed. She was about to give him a piece of her mind when Jack jerked his thumb toward the Webcam. He didn't think it was there for security reasons. And those babies carried picture and sound.

She caught his signal like a pro. "Jack, I shouldn't have let you talk me into coming here. I've changed my mind. I just can't…"

"I've already paid the man." Jack took her hand

and squeezed it. ''I don't think he's going to give me my money back.''

''I'll make it up to you later, sweetie pie. Just get me out of here. All this black stuff gives me the creeps.''

''But—''

''Pretty please? My mother surfs the Net. If she ever saw me, us, well, she'd probably cut me out of her will then go straight to her grave.''

''All right. Okay,'' Jack agreed, pleased that she'd understood exactly what he'd needed. Together they walked down the stairs.

Just as he'd expected, Easy had been listening to their conversation. He folded his arms over his huge chest, blocking their way out. ''I don't give refunds.''

The man hadn't even pretended not to be spying on them. Interesting.

Jack didn't care about the money, but if he didn't furnish a token protest the man might become suspicious. Although Easy's computer records made him appear innocent, Jack saw no reason to enlighten him—especially when he clearly wasn't going to cooperate. ''How about a rain check?''

''Pest ain't changing her mind.''

Piper glared at Easy. ''My mom brought me up better.''

Jack frowned at her. ''What if I come back—''

''With another partner?'' Easy sneered at Piper. ''Then, yeah. You can have a rain check, dude.''

''Thanks.'' The men shook hands.

Piper sighed a shudder of relief that went right through his arm, which was around her waist, as they exited the house. ''What a sleazebag.''

''A rich sleazebag.''

''What exactly does he do?''

''He rents rooms to couples. Digitalizes their activities, records them on a CD-ROM and offers the video stream for sale on the Internet. He gets a cut of every download.''

''I'm glad you arrived when you did.'' Piper threw her arms around his neck and kissed him. ''My hero.''

He should have stopped her, but he didn't have the willpower. So he drew her close, breathed in her sooty scent and planted kisses on her lips. ''I seriously doubt you needed help.''

She kissed him back, flattening her body against his, melding their mouths, giving him her heat. Her hands were sliding over his shoulders, down his back, his buttocks.

She tilted her head back. ''Nothing would have pleased me more than to kick him where it would hurt the most,'' she whispered into his mouth. ''That look in his eyes was sick.'' She shivered, her breasts pressed against his chest, her hips rubbing his as if to get warm.

Naturally his body again responded to her being pressed so close to him. In self-defense he gently pulled away. Intentionally or not, she was playing him like a yo-yo. And he could take only so much.

''I didn't find a thing on his computer system to

link him to your firing or the arson,'' Jack told her
once they were in the car. He'd had to sit slowly or
risk cutting off his circulation. ''But his fire wall was
way above average. I have to give him an A for effort.''

''He's clean?'' Disappointment clouded her voice.
She sagged in her seat and her shoulders slumped.
''What now?''

''We'll track down more of your father's old students and take a closer look at Danna Mudd's and
Aaron Hodges's backgrounds. Maybe talk to Venus
again. She might be willing to tell us more, now that
Leroy is beyond the reach of the law. And Leroy's
wife might know something, too. But I'd rather give
her a few days to bury her husband before we question
her.''

''Agreed. And I want to shower and change clothes
before we talk to anyone else. Is it safe to go to my
folks' house or a hotel?''

Jack would have preferred to work through the
night. Preferably not in a hotel. Not with Piper next
door. But he couldn't think of a solid reason to deny
her the comfort of a hot shower and a bed—except
that he could no longer remember why he was resist-
ing her advances. It might have something to do with
the fact that after her kiss, he no longer had any blood
above the waist.

''We aren't going back to your folks' house until
we solve this case. I can access the equipment at their

house from a new hotel.'' Despite his effort to speak in a normal tone, his voice was husky with desire.

''Fine.'' She patted his leg and let her fingers trail up his thigh. ''This time we'll just need one room.''

HOW DARE THEY COME to the place of business?

No wonder the e-mails from the buyers had stopped. In a high-caliber operation like this one, nobody could afford to make a mistake. Between the new agency of Homeland Security and the combined forces of the CIA and FBI scouring the country for terrorists, pulling off a scheme so bold would make all but the bravest of men hide at the first sign of trouble.

The damn cop and her double-damn lover boy were doing real harm. They had to be stopped.

Wait.

Think outside the box.

The operation needn't be run from here.

There was no reason not to go, leave everything behind. Not with the riches waiting at the end of the rainbow.

Fingers flew over the keyboard. "Setting up in new location."

The reply came back almost instantly. "That would be wise. Is the information secure?"

"Of course. What about my payment?"

"Ready and waiting."

"Then we are good to go. Give me forty-eight hours."

"Twenty-four."

"Thirty-six."

"Done."

"Take the utmost care. The consequences of failure are permanent."

A threat? Or a warning? It didn't matter.

Disappearing wasn't hard. Not when one knew how to steal an ID off the Internet. Not when one could work in cash. Not for someone with an IQ of 176 and the guts to match.

Let Payne and Donovan search all they wanted. By the time they figured out what had happened, it would be too late.

Chapter Eleven

Jack tossed the luggage onto the bed. "You can hit the shower first."

"Why don't we share the hot water?" Piper rested her hand on a cocked hip and gave him a saucy smile that curled his toes.

Ever since he'd registered for only one room, an aura of supreme confidence seemed to have surrounded her. Nothing he said, none of his most ferocious scowls made the least bit of difference in her attitude.

"I need to set up the computer. Compile notes on Aaron Hodges, Danna Mudd and Easy As Pie for Adam to profile. With more specific data he might narrow down the suspects for us even further."

And Jack needed to cool down. She might be ready. But he was over ready.

She'd kept him off balance all day. His entire body was set to boil over and he desperately needed to simmer down. Regain a measure of control. Distance would do the trick.

If she'd just go into the bathroom. Give him a few precious minutes for his body to recuperate. His mind to settle. His stomach to unknot.

Piper didn't argue. She just stripped—her shirt, her bra, her pants, her panties. Until she stood naked. Right there in the middle of the room.

He'd never seen anyone so beautiful. She had delicate breasts that puckered into hard tips, a flat tummy and slender hips, but it was her free spirit that seized hold of his heart.

His entire body clenched and his mind froze in got-to-have-her mode as he stared in wonder, appreciation and awe. Her breasts rose high on her chest and her nipples, tiny rosebuds, bloomed under his gaze. His jeans grew so tight the seam must have been making a permanent indentation.

He'd seen her nude before—in the dark. With the hotel room's lights showing off her perfect sun-kissed tan and emphasizing her breasts and the tiny triangle between her thighs, his blood rushed south. Quite simply, he couldn't have resisted her for another hour, never mind another day.

That he'd once tried to deny her potent attraction now seemed the height of idiocy. What had he been thinking?

She was all woman. She was willing. And waiting. For him.

"I didn't do it right, did I?" she muttered.

His mouth felt sand dry with need, so he could barely get words past his tongue. "Do what right?"

"Strip. I was going to tease you. Take my time. But I forgot the plan."

"You don't honestly think I'm going to complain about the way you took off your clothes?"

"Then why are you just standing there staring at me? Shouldn't you be *doing* something?"

"I'm staring because you are delectable and tempting and if I come any closer—"

She flew across the room and straight into his arms, tumbling him onto the bed, landing on top of him with a soft *oof.*

I'm going to explode.

"Kiss me, Jack."

He twisted his hips, preventing permanent damage. "Whoa, babe. You've got to slow down."

She squirmed against him. "I've been waiting twenty-five years to make love. I don't want to wait another second."

He threaded his fingers into her hair, pulled back her head so he could gaze deep into her eyes. "You've never?"

She shook her head. "But I'm sure."

When a man was offered such a precious gift, he didn't ask questions. Not when the lady was tearing the buttons off his shirt in order to slide her naked flesh against his eager chest.

His cell phone rang and he bit back a curse of frustration. "I need to answer that."

"Kiss me first."

He kissed her and pressed the receive button on his

phone. But he couldn't speak as she blew him away with a storm of passion. His lips explored hers, their tongues entwined until his blood thundered and his heart roared.

''Hello. Hello.'' A voice came from his phone.

Somehow he found the will to break their lip lock. Piper simply traded his lips for his ear. Her light nips stung, but then she took away the pain with tiny licks that made him consider turning off his phone's power. Surely his battery could go dead every once in a while?

Except Logan had packed spare batteries. And missing a phone call from headquarters or another team member could put a life at risk.

He checked caller ID. He'd never hoped for a wrong number so badly in his life.

Jack wanted to shout, ''Not now'' at the caller from the Shey Group's home office. He settled for a husky ''Yes.''

Piper had abandoned his ear. Her tongue swirled over his nipple and her hands were everywhere, seeking, stroking, seducing.

Perhaps the phone call's distraction would help cool him down. Jack held the phone to his ear.

''The stolen cell phone hasn't been used,'' Ryker Stevens told him. Ryker might be a brilliant computer hacker, but his timing sucked.

Piper's greedy hands were unbuttoning Jack's fly. But he couldn't let her touch him or he'd lose it. ''Not yet.''

Ryker, on the other end of his phone, must have thought Jack had been talking to him. "You don't need a pen and paper. This isn't rocket science."

Jack couldn't counter Piper's moves with just one hand. She had his jeans unbuttoned. He needed to get off the phone, and he grunted, "Huh?"

"Leroy's wife's cell phone. You wanted me to check to see if any calls had been—"

"Okay, thanks." He cut off Ryker and made a mental note to thank him again and apologize for his rudeness later.

Piper had just removed his jeans and tossed them to the floor when Jack sat up and tugged her onto the bed, then rolled her to her back and settled between her thighs. He used his body to pin her on the bed. "Slow down. There's no rush."

She never did listen worth a damn. Her hands slipped down his sides and into his briefs.

"I've waited way too long, Jack. I don't want to waste any more time."

"You should let me take the lead."

She rolled her eyes toward the ceiling. "If I waited for you to lead, we'd never get anywhere."

"Hey, I'm the one who knows what he's doing."

"If you knew what you were doing, you'd be putting your mouth to better use than arguing with me," she teased.

"Exactly where do you want my mouth?" He kissed her chin. "Here?" He kissed her collarbone.

"Here?" He dipped his head to kiss her navel. "Or maybe here?"

She rose on her elbows, her breasts heaving. "I thought you said you knew what you were doing."

"I do." He sat back on his heels, unsure whether to be amused or insulted.

"Well, there's a bunch of spots between my shoulders and my waist that you neglected."

He grinned at her bossy impatience. "Nag. Nag. Nag."

She chuckled. "And why aren't you naked? In case you're shy—"

"I'm not shy."

"—let me remind you that I've already seen you in the nude."

There was really only one way to shut her up. He eased back over her and kissed her mouth. She might be a virgin, but she sure knew how to kiss like a dream. And she put her whole body into the kiss, wrapping her arms around his back, threading her fingers into his hair, pressing her breasts against his chest.

As if on cue, his phone rang again.

Damn. What was he? Mr. Popularity all of a sudden?

She groaned, then pulled her mouth free. "Don't answer it."

"Got to." He felt around on the bed, found the phone and checked the caller ID. "It's Adam."

"Who?"

"Our profiler. Just let me tell him that I'll call him back."

She snatched the ringing phone from his hand.

Jack narrowed his eyes as she held the phone over the edge of the bed and out of his reach. "Hey. Give me that."

"No."

"Might be important."

Her eyes gleamed with mischievous heat. "I'll trade you the phone for your briefs."

One more ring and voice mail would pick up. He gave in. "Fine."

She tossed him the phone. And her hands shoved down his last physical defense against her.

Out of necessity, Jack needed to keep the call short. "Adam, I've got to—"

"Listen to me."

Piper's hand closed around Jack's erection.

She didn't understand that she was going to push him over the edge. But his tone came out harsher than he'd intended. "No."

"Don't tell me no," Adam said.

She skimmed her hands up and down over his sex. Sweat beaded his brow. "I wasn't talking to you."

Piper grinned. "Oh, you're *talking* to me, all right."

"Did I call at a bad time?" Adam asked.

"No." Yeah. Couldn't have been worse. He felt like shouting into the receiver that he was being seduced by a virgin. He could just imagine Adam's face.

But then he'd have to make explanations, which he didn't want to do.

Not when she felt so good.

But she had to stop. Jack already felt as though he couldn't hold on another second.

Normally he had more control. But she'd had him up and down all day. And she was—oh, my—her curiosity was killing him, slowly. She had no mercy. No idea of—

"Do you have any more information for me to add to the profile?"

"Adam, if this isn't an emergency, then I really can't talk now."

"But you just said—"

"Call...you...back...soon."

He reached down to draw her up to him for another kiss. "Piper, honey, you've got to stop."

"Okay." She kept right on doing what she'd been doing. Driving him crazy with need.

"I mean it. You've got to—" His cell phone rang again. Every atom in his body wanted to hurl the phone across the room. But when his legendary boss called, the man whose influence reached from the White House to the Kremlin, one didn't ignore the call.

"Go on, answer the phone," Piper told him with a chuckle, her hands quite busy. "Don't let me interrupt."

"Yes," he answered. Naturally she took that as permission to stroke him however she liked.

"You okay?" Logan asked.

"Yes."

Her hands moved faster.

"Well, you just hung up with—"

"I know. Can this wait, sir?"

"Are you in trouble, Jack?"

He was in so much trouble his head was spinning. "Not the kind you have to worry about." And then she replaced her hands with her mouth.

"You're sure?"

Piper paused long enough to say, "We have our clothes off again."

Logan chuckled.

Jack barely bit back a groan. He was dying here. Dying and flying and about to crash and burn. "Let me call you back, okay?" And he hung up.

But he could no longer pull away. She'd gone too far and he couldn't... He exploded in the most sensational orgasm ever.

Blood pounded through his head. And somewhere through the haze of pleasure he could see Piper frowning at him.

"Jack, you aren't supposed to... You can't..."

But he had. "Damn it. Why wouldn't you listen?"

Piper groaned and dropped her face onto the blanket. "I'm sorry. You have no idea how much. I've been waiting twenty-five years to make love and I just blew it, didn't I?"

"Actually, I blew it." Gently he cradled her in his

arms, her head tucked under his chin. "You know what's the best thing about making love?"

"How would I know?"

"Practice makes perfect."

"Okay."

"And I wanted you so badly, I just couldn't wait. Not with what you were doing to me," he admitted.

She snuggled against him. "Oh, Jack."

"We went about this all backward. Give me a few minutes to recover and—"

"And?"

He snapped his fingers. "Talk about doing things *backward*. I just had a most incredible idea."

"About making love?"

"No, about solving your case."

STILL MORTIFIED by her overzealous behavior, Piper slipped into a robe and belted it tight. Jack hadn't bothered to don so much as his briefs.

He plugged in his computer and typed like a man on a mission. "I instructed the computer to look in the wrong area. I was assuming someone paid Vince and Leroy to lie about you. So the computer was looking for deposits into their accounts. But Vince's mother told us he was broke and Venus told us the same thing about Leroy."

"So?"

"So suppose someone was blackmailing them?" Jack typed as he spoke.

She couldn't read the codes he was typing, but his

words shot a slew of possibilities at her. Yet she was still having trouble thinking about the case. She couldn't so easily put aside what had just happened between them.

Had Jack wanted her as badly as he'd claimed? Or was he using the excuse to make her feel better?

"This may be the break we needed, thanks to you."

"I didn't do anything."

"Without you, I wouldn't have thought to see if regular payments might be coming *out* of both Vince's and Leroy's accounts." He pointed to the screen. "Look."

"Vince wrote a check on the first of the month to Cayman Islands National Bank." She leaned forward as he split the screen. "Ditto for Leroy. We have our connection."

"Right. They were both being blackmailed, but by whom?" His fingers danced on the keyboard, his movements a blur.

"Tell me you aren't hacking into a bank in the Cayman Islands?"

"I'm asking Logan for permission to have Ryker Stevens do it. I'm good—but he's better. For international hacks, I leave the fun to him."

"Fun?"

"Besides, he won't get caught. He knows how to cover his tracks better than I do."

"So." She folded her arms across her chest. "You have no more work to do?"

"None at the keyboard."

She slid onto his lap. "Didn't you say something about practice makes perfect?"

"Did I say that?" he teased.

"You also said that if I slowed down you would take the lead. Well, lead on, Jack."

He reached inside her robe and cupped her breasts. "Nag. Nag. Nag."

She had to fight her every natural instinct to tell him to hurry. But he wanted to explore her every curve with a thoroughness that had her clenching her teeth to keep from telling him that for a guy who liked speed, he sure was going mighty slowly.

He tweaked her nipples, and just as fire shot through her, he stood, taking her to her feet with him. "What about that shower?"

She narrowed her eyes. "Do we get to wash each other?"

"Nope."

"Then—"

"Not unless I decide to let you."

A shiver of yearning swept straight to her core. "But—"

"This time we do things my way."

"Okay."

"That means you will let me set the pace."

"Okay."

"And I do the touching."

A rush of heat between her thighs told her that the night was still young. "Fine."

"This time you will be at *my* mercy," he promised.

She swallowed hard in anticipation. "I don't get to do anything?"

"Nothing, except think about what I'm going to do to you next."

As a cop, Piper was all too accustomed to making decisions, acting and following through. She hadn't had experience in giving herself up to anyone, not for any reason. What Jack was asking her to do required an enormous amount of trust.

And that's when it hit her like a runaway truck. She wouldn't even have considered his suggestion if she didn't already love Jack. She trusted him, loved him. And perhaps she always had.

The idea stunned her into momentary silence, but the idea of loving Jack felt so right that she knew she would do exactly as he asked. Not because he was more experienced. Not even because he'd asked it of her.

But because she loved him.

Jack laced her fingers through his, and together they entered the bathroom. He adjusted the hot water and then held out his hand to help her step over the tub's rim. The gesture, so gallant in nature, was all Jack. So was the pleasure in his eyes as he positioned her under the spray of water.

She tilted back her head. Water cascaded over her forehead, down her cheeks and her neck to her breasts.

"Turn around. I'll wash your hair."

His fingers on her scalp felt great, matching the

warm and fuzzy feeling inside that she was still holding so close. She was in love.

She supposed loving Jack shouldn't have come as such a surprise. As a teenager, she'd always compared her dates to Jack. And somehow they never measured up.

He was one of a kind. What other speed demon could slow down enough to wash a woman's hair? Or to take such pleasure in nipping the curves of her neck with his mouth, regardless of the water splashing on his face?

"Rinse." He directed her under the water, and she closed her eyes, giving herself up to his ministrations. "Conditioner?"

"Yes, please."

He worked in the rinse slowly, as if his fingers would never tire of playing with her hair. As if he had nothing more pressing to do than to make sure he dispersed the rinse evenly.

And for once, his phone remained silent. Thank goodness for small favors.

"Let's see. What part of you should I wash next?" His tone was husky. She had to will herself not to lean into him, throw her arms around his neck and kiss him.

The tender newness of her feelings caused her to want to sing from the rooftop, shout her happiness to the world.

"I suppose it's only logical to wash away the soot from the top down." Jack's statement indicated that he was merely solving a puzzle, like how to dismantle an engine or piece together his computer code—except for the edge of hunger in his tone.

He soaped her back, her breasts, her belly and her legs. He didn't tease or spend more time on the erogenous zones. And by his doing so, she felt pampered and cherished as a whole person. Happiness cloaked her in a bubble that she wouldn't allow to burst. She didn't think of yesterday or tomorrow. There was only now. This perfect moment with Jack.

He switched places with her and she watched him shower. He washed his hair, using half the amount of shampoo she'd needed. From a travel pack he plucked out a razor and gel. Watching him shave seemed more intimate than being naked together.

When their eyes caught, he grinned. "You cold?"

She shook her head, fascinated how the heat in his eyes could lick down her spine and warm her from her front to her back. "I don't think I've ever seen a man shave before. It's rather…sexy."

"Tonight will get better."

"Jack. There's something I just figured out."

"Can it wait?"

"It's not about the case."

"Okay."

"I love you."

He looked at her. "Okay."

She placed her hands on her hips. "That's all you can say? Okay?"

"I may not be the most insightful guy in the world,

but somehow I guessed you wouldn't be about to make love unless you cared about me.''

"And?''

He tossed her the soap. "Wash my back?''

Wash his back? She wanted to heave the soap in his face in the same way he'd thrown her love back in her face. But she didn't.

Just because she loved him didn't necessarily mean he loved her. How could she have forgotten such an elementary law of nature?

Obviously Jack found her attractive. She believed that he liked her a lot. He'd proved that she mattered to him. As a friend. A good friend. Or he might have lied to her and said he loved her when he didn't—but he hadn't. She couldn't fault him for his honesty.

When he turned his back, she washed him, letting her hands enjoy the hard muscles beneath his warm flesh, allowing her fingers to memorize the angles and planes of his shoulders and spine. Was he deliberately giving her time to change her mind?

Did she want to make love to a man who didn't love her? Most of her colleagues and friends on the force would have laughed in her face at such an old-fashioned moral question. In this day and age, where kids often lost their virginity by age sixteen, she'd held on to her ideals for close to a decade longer than the average. But she hadn't made her decision based on statistics and averages. Making love or not had never been a hard decision—until now.

Maybe she was a late bloomer, or just content with

her own life—enough to wait for the right moment—
but she'd never been really tempted. Until Jack.

Even knowing he didn't reciprocate her feelings,
even knowing that this night might be their only time
together—for her, it was right. She couldn't control
his feelings, only her own. And she had no reason not
to trust her instincts. After all, she hadn't made a bad
lovemaking decision yet. She grinned. And threw
away her caution.

Right now Jack was the right man for her. He was
good and honest. And she didn't want to wait. Not
another decade, not another year. Not another day.

"Jack."

"You feel great."

"Jack."

"Yeah."

"I still want you."

"I want you, too," he admitted.

And for now that would have to be enough.

He turned and took her into his arms and just held
her against him under the water. She had never felt so
safe and excited at the same time. Standing in his em-
brace was heaven. So why was it so hard for her to
hold still?

Why did she want more? More of his mouth on
hers. More than his arms wrapped around her.

She trembled, but he didn't need to ask if she was
cold. He could feel her heat against his, her heart
thumping out of control, just as she could take comfort
in the strong steady beat of his.

No matter what happened, she never wanted to forget this moment. Didn't want to forget how Jack made her believe in herself. She had no idea how long they stood together under the water, but when they finally left the shower, her fingertips were puckered.

And she knew without a doubt that she would never regret being with Jack—no matter what happened between them next.

Chapter Twelve

Jack usually took his sex like his morning newspaper. He skimmed the parts of little interest like the comics and the home and garden sections and delved into news and sports. With Piper, he didn't want to skim over chitchat, or kissing or exploring every inch of her before moving on. There was no part of making love with her that he wanted to skimp on.

Instead he intended to savor and prolong the experience. For her. And for him. But more for her.

This was her first time. And he was determined to make everything right and beautiful for her. She deserved to have that much from him.

Jack draped a towel over the commode, gestured for her to sit and rubbed her hair dry with another towel. Then he used his fingers for a comb and let the blow-dryer finish the job. He took his time, enjoying the feel of her silky hair sliding through his fingers. He liked the deep auburn color, the rich shimmer under the lights, the contact of his fingertips on her scalp.

When her hair was dry, she appeared fluffy. Jack

replaced the blow-dryer in the holder on the wall, then held out his hand to her. She didn't hesitate to take it, and rose to her feet with a grace that made his mouth water. With her cheeks pink and flushed from the heat of the dryer and her eyes dilated to the max, she had the look of some fairy sprite, all smooth ivory flesh and pink-tipped breasts.

Without a kiss or one erotic touch, his sex had reloaded and was again ready to fire. But with the edge off, he could wait. This was going to be good for her.

"What are you thinking?" she asked.

"How much I want you."

She glanced down at his erection and her words floated to him on a sexy giggle. "I can see that."

"And this time you aren't going to touch me. Not until I'm inside you." He led her to the bed, swept away the spread and blanket, eased her back onto the cool crisp sheets. She drew him down and he shifted his hips to lie by her side.

Like a feast laid out for him to relish, she couldn't have pleased him more. When he did no more than look at her, her nipples hardened to ripe buds. At her response to just his glance, his hunger deepened. He fisted his hand in her hair, turned her head until he could reach her mouth. She parted her lips, but waited for him to deepen the kiss, holding up her end of their bargain.

He nibbled and nipped. And while they kissed, he cupped her jaw, traced her collarbone, circled her breasts, teasing and taunting but not quite touching until he elicited a soft moan from the back of her throat.

"Too slow," she complained.

"There's no hurry. We have all night."

She stared at him, her pupils dilated, her breath ragged. "I don't want to wait."

"Shh." He kissed the tip of her breast. "You don't know what you want."

"I want more of that," she demanded.

And he complied, swirling his tongue over her. When she arched her back and her legs parted, he skimmed his fingers up and down her thighs, occasionally dipping to the tender flesh inside her knees.

"Jack."

"Yeah?"

"I feel…light-headed."

"You're supposed to."

"I can't seem to catch my breath."

"Good."

He touched the insides of her thighs.

"I've got to…to…to…"

"You've got nothing to do except wait. Wait to see where I touch you next, remember?"

She sighed. "How can I think when…"

He kissed her mouth, a lush mouth, pouting for him. A mouth that gave him so much pleasure. At the same time they kissed, he touched between her legs. She was damp, slick and so ready she moaned into his mouth. Parting her legs wider, she invited him to touch, to tease and to stroke and he found her openness both sexy and poignant.

Some other time he would make her wait longer, take her to the edge and back, drive her crazy with need until she was wild with wanting. But this first time he would give her all the tenderness he could. He wanted this experience to be wondrous and gentle and exciting for her more than he wanted his own pleasure. He would not overwhelm her to prove he had the skill to do so.

Jack knew the next stage would be tricky. She was bound to be tight, and he didn't want to cause her any pain at all.

He took his time, placing one finger inside her, then two, allowing her to accustom herself to him. Every single cell in his body demanded that he take her now, delve into her heat.

He'd never known holding back could be so difficult. He had no idea how Piper made him feel both protective and hot at the same time, but she did.

Jack tore open a foil packet, rolled the condom over his sex and reminded himself that going slowly was critical. As much as his body demanded to plunge into her, he would hold back.

Gritting his teeth, he positioned himself between her legs.

"Jack?"

Of all times, leave it to Piper to question him now. "What?"

"You look like you're in pain. Isn't this supposed to be fun?"

Jack groaned into her neck and let the tip of his sex nestle between her thighs. That she could worry over him at a time like this shook him to his core.

"I want you…so much." He smoothed back her hair and gazed into her eyes as slowly he moved into her heat. He'd expected resistance. There was none. He'd expected heat. There was plenty. He'd expected to feel good—but not this good.

"I'm fine, Jack. Now, quit your worrying and show a girl a good time."

She knew exactly what to say to kick in his instincts. Still, he moved slowly, letting her body adjust to the feel of him. At the same time he reached between her thighs, giving her more sensations, more pleasure. And she responded by wrapping her arms around his neck and moving her hips.

"This is…good," she muttered. "So…so…ohh."

And as if perfectly planned and accomplished, together they found joy in one another. She spasmed around him, increasing his own pleasure. When he could think again, he wrapped her in his arms, snuggled her head against his chest and held her with a contentment he'd rarely known.

THEY MADE LOVE AGAIN in the morning, and she slept, then awakened refreshed and not the tiniest bit sore—thanks to Jack. He'd been incredibly tender. Making love to him had been beyond incredible, more than worth waiting for. In fact, if he hadn't had such dark circles under his eyes, she might have tried to lure him back to bed.

Jack was working. He stared bleary-eyed at the laptop's screen, and guilt stabbed her. He'd stayed awake part of the night, working on her behalf while she'd slept alone. And she'd been so pleasantly exhausted she hadn't noticed the light from his screen, his tapping on the keyboard or his making coffee.

Beside his makeshift desk sat an empty coffee cup and a pad of notepaper with scribbles all over it. She slid out of bed, wrapped the top sheet around her and placed her hands on Jack's knotted shoulders.

He glanced up at her and grinned a sexy grin that made her heart turn a cartwheel. "Morning."

"Morning, yourself." She dug her fingers deeper into his tendons, which were tensed from keyboarding fatigue. The way his muscles bunched, he could have been hanging plasterboard all night.

He leaned his head back against her belly. "Mmm. I'll give you an hour to stop that."

"Do we have an hour?" Maybe he wasn't as tired as he appeared. "Because if we do, I know a better way to—"

"Actually, we have to get out of here soon." He looked inordinately pleased with himself. And while she preferred to believe that their lovemaking had made his face light up and his eyes glint, she suspected he'd finally figured out her problem.

Excitement layered over her previous contentment. "You solved the case?"

"Give me a kiss and I'll tell you." He tugged her into his lap.

"Tell me and you'll get more than a kiss." She kissed his mouth and snuggled into him.

"Well, Vince and Leroy were being blackmailed, all right. Their checks both ended up in the same account in the Cayman Islands. Actually, lots of people with nothing to do with your case were being blackmailed. Some paid weekly. Some monthly. I suspect the blackmailer used the Internet to find illicit behavior and then contacted the cheaters. Leroy was cheating on his wife. Vince was taking kickbacks from suppliers."

"So the blackmailer used that information against them to get to me?"

"As far as I can tell, yes."

"Okay, whose account is it?"

"The account belongs to a subsidiary of a Costa Rican corporation."

She appreciated his hard work, she really did. However, she wished he would just tell her already. "Who owns the corporation?"

"Hodges Computer Systems. And Aaron was in the Costa Rican military, which explains how he learned about bugs and bombs."

She jumped off his lap. "Aaron Hodges is the guy? I don't understand. Why would he set up such an elaborate scheme to get me fired?"

"I'm getting to that. Would you like a cup of coffee? You're a little cranky in the morning," Jack teased.

"Yes to the coffee. And I'm not cranky," she denied. Still, she refrained from asking him another question until she'd swallowed two sips of lukewarm coffee. "You look quite pleased with yourself."

"Maybe that's due to making love to you." He was still teasing her, and she tried to be patient, but patience wasn't one of her better qualities. However, the last time she'd been impatient and had acted precipitously, she'd ruined their first shot at lovemaking. The painful memory still made her wince, though Jack had replaced her mistake with much better memories.

"What did you find?" she prodded.

"Aaron Hodges is a busy man."

She frowned at him over the rim of her cup. "He runs his own computer company. Of course he's busy."

"Hodges Computer Systems isn't making any money. He's in the red. In fact, he had to put a hundred grand of the money he earned from blackmailing into the company last year to keep it running."

Okay. She understood he was following the money trail, but she had no idea where he was going. "So how did I get in Aaron Hodges's way?"

"He hacked into the Department of Defense."

"Excuse me?" She rubbed her forehead in confusion. "What did you say?"

"Ryker's program put a trace on the hack. We've

got Aaron Hodges nailed for hacking into the Defense Department.''

"You're saying Aaron was selling information from our government to—"

"The highest bidder. Anyone who can hack into the DOD would consider getting into the police department's mainframe the equivalent of kindergarten play."

"But why did he come after me?"

"I'm guessing that your investigation into the fire at your parents' home made him nervous. Maybe scared away customers. Criminals don't like it when a cop's interested in them."

"So I was just the small fry caught up in Aaron's master plan?" She worked out the details and sighed. "I'll bet he's also responsible for the university virus and for torching my folks' house."

"I can't think of another reason he would have gone after you. But he's got bigger things to worry about now than arson, bribery and blackmail charges. Like spending his life in jail for treason. You've helped uncover a spy."

"You did all the work."

"You helped. The important thing is that you're going to get your job back."

She wanted to celebrate but held back, sensing he had more to tell her. "Why do I sense a but coming?"

"There's just one tiny problem," he admitted.

"What?"

"Aaron Hodges has disappeared."

"How do you know?"

"I've brought in part of the Shey Group to help us. Web's been watching his home. Travis is at the store. Aaron's not there. Logan's alerted law enforcement, both local and state police. The airports are being watched. Don't worry, we'll find him."

Piper wasn't so sure. A man like Aaron Hodges who had the resources of the Internet at his command could disappear with a fake identity. He could crawl into a hole in South America or Africa and never be seen again. While the evidence Jack had found would probably clear her name and get back her job, her fears escalated.

"Jack."

"Yeah."

"What kind of information did he steal from the Defense Department?"

"I can't tell you that."

"You don't know? Wouldn't the computer trace—"

Jack shook his head. "It's classified. And suffice it to say that Logan Kincaid has already informed the FBI, the CIA and the president—"

"The president?" She sank onto the bed, her knees weak. "The stolen information is that serious?"

"Yeah."

AARON HODGES HAD an escape plan. But he hadn't planned to leave so quickly. Hadn't expected his opponents to mobilize their forces within hours.

Still, he patted his laptop and the CD-ROM with the critical information on it that would soon make him rich. He'd be fine. All he needed to complete his transaction was a cell phone and a drop box.

Damn Payne for bringing the Shey Group onto his trail. He should have killed her earlier—a slight miscalculation on his part that he could still rectify. That woman would not be allowed to chase him out of his home and business and then get away scot-free. Oh, no. Even his masterful escape plan had time for revenge.

Payne would die. Perhaps too quickly. He would have preferred her to suffer longer, die painfully after all her interference. But he would have to satisfy himself with all the lovely money he was about to collect when he sold his information.

Besides, the business had become a drag. His new life would be more exciting. And his new wealth would buy him everything he desired. Now all he had to do was set his trap. And keep going.

"HOW ARE WE GOING TO FIND Aaron? And why do we want to? Shouldn't the government take over now?'' Piper asked Jack as they checked out of the hotel. She was amazed at the amount of information he'd uncovered in such a short time. But she knew from her work as a detective that investigations often were full of dead ends and seemingly useless bits of information—

and then *kapow*. The pieces would coalesce into one cohesive whole, allowing her to see the big picture.

It was just too bad Hodges always seemed one step ahead of them. She didn't have a good feeling about today. Perhaps the grim sky and thunderclouds had something to do with her churning emotions.

"Logan Kincaid has sent the new information to his contacts. The Shey Group is no longer working pro bono. We've been paid to catch Aaron Hodges and to keep the information quiet."

"But why can't government authorities take over the job of catching him?"

"Because the Shey Group can keep its operations out of the press. And we don't have to report to government committees. If we can capture Aaron, it's possible we can turn him and learn about his contacts."

"But we have no idea where he is."

"I have an idea." Jack threw their baggage into the car trunk and slammed down the lid. "Do you remember the pictures of Aaron on the wall in his office?"

"Yeah. He was hunting and golfing and…fishing." Piper snapped her fingers. "He has a boat!"

"Logan already has the Coast Guard searching, but the Gulf of Mexico and Tampa Bay have a lot of water and coves to cover. I thought we'd take up the helicopter and add our eyes to the search."

Take up the chopper? She looked out the window and imagined that the waves in Tampa Bay would be almost as choppy as in the Gulf. Forecasters might have issued small craft warnings. And the winds had to be gusting upward of fifteen knots. Not exactly good boating or good flying weather. But she'd already slept while Jack worked through part of the night—she wouldn't let him fly alone. Even if her only job was to keep him awake in the pilot's seat, she would go—just to do that.

"You think you know where Aaron went?" she asked him.

"In the picture there was a small island in the distance and a plane in the sky. I'm betting he was in the bay at the time, either in MacDill Air Force Base's flight pattern or Tampa International's."

"But why would he go to the same spot now? He's either hiding or fleeing."

Jack shrugged. "It's only a place to start. But people tend to stick to predictable patterns. On the water he'll naturally follow his usual routes as much as possible."

"Makes sense." She didn't say more. Just watched Jack drive through the traffic and frowned at the darkening sky. She flipped on the radio and caught a weather report.

Intermittent thunderstorms. Typical Floridian summer. She refused to think about the common waterspouts and tornadoes, which could fling a helicopter from the sky. The military had trained Jack to be a superb pilot and he wouldn't take her up if he considered the situation dangerous.

Still, she'd never flown in a helicopter. And the occasional lightning strikes zapping from sky to land and back weren't comforting.

When Jack drove into the small airport, he did what to her looked like a thorough preflight check. She sat in the copilot's seat and tightened her seat belt. With only a thin sheet of Plexiglas between her and thin air, she didn't look down.

Jack handed her a headset, and she placed it over her ears and adjusted the microphone near her lips. The headphones cut the noise of the engines and rotors, so when Jack suddenly said, "All set?" she could hear him as easily as if they'd been in the car.

"Yes."

"We'll head across the peninsula and east toward Tampa Bay."

Jack maneuvered the helicopter out of the protective shed, then rose straight up. Her stomach soared into her throat. She clutched the arms of her seat so tightly that her fingertips hurt.

A gust of wind produced a little wobble. She let out a startled gasp.

"Sorry about that." Jack compensated, using both hands and feet to maneuver, a delighted grin on his face. "The bumps remind me of rides in the amusement park."

He was having fun.

Clearly they were in no danger.

She forced her fingertips to relax. Forced herself to breathe.

She was a good flyer. Didn't mind even commuter planes with props.

She glanced down.

Big mistake.

The sensation wasn't like flying in an airplane where one's body was surrounded by metal with tiny windows to look out. There were clouds inches from her feet. And the helicopter seemed no more substantial to her than a bubble.

Get over it.

Last night Jack had taught her how to make love and she'd thoroughly enjoyed herself. She was glad she'd put herself into his capable hands. Those same hands were now piloting the chopper, and while she trusted his piloting abilities and his judgment, she still couldn't quiet her nerves. However, with practice, she could learn to perch above the earth like a bird, learn to ignore the sickening lurch in her stomach, learn to ignore the fact that if one tiny piece of equipment malfunctioned then they would plummet to their deaths.

In a few more minutes maybe she'd even stop shaking.

All too soon they were no longer over land, but following the Howard Frankland Bridge from Clearwater to Tampa. She could see the Tampa Bay Buccaneers' stadium. The international airport. A cruise ship docked at the aquarium.

"There's Davis Island and MacDill." Jack pointed, apparently oblivious to her case of nerves. "We'll give their airspace a wide berth and head toward Sarasota and the Skyway Bridge.''

While he banked into a smooth turn, she managed to breathe almost normally. Proud of herself, she risked another glance down and realized they were much lower. The crests of the waves below were bigger. She could make out several fishing boats—all heading back to port.

She didn't know if the Coast Guard had helicopters, but she could understand why Jack had wanted to search from the air. They could cover a lot of open water quickly. And with the bad weather, there were not that many small boats out. A few hardy sailors taking advantage of the wind. Oceangoing ships in the channel and sea-lanes. Tugs guiding barges into the port.

And she could make out a school of dolphins frolicking in the waves below. Fascinated, she pointed. "Look."

"Cool, huh?" Jack dropped lower for a better look. "I've seen manatees and the occasional whale in the Gulf. And always lots of sharks."

Damn it. Why did he have to go and remind her of the sharks that frequented these waters? She preferred not to think about them ever. After seeing the movie *Jaws* as a kid, it had taken her two whole summers to swim at the beach.

"There!" Jack pointed to a boat heading straight toward the Skyway Bridge and the Gulf of Mexico. "She sure looks like the boat in that picture."

"How can you tell from here?" she asked, then wished she'd just kept her mouth shut. To her there were ships and tugboats, powerboats and sailboats, and this particular boat looked like every other cabin cruiser in the bay.

"The shape of the hull is different. So are the portholes. If you'll get my pack—" Jack jerked his thumb toward the seats two rows back "—there's a pair of binoculars that should help us."

She had to remove her headset, since the wires kept her bound to the front seat. Squeezing between the seats, she reached for the pack he'd tossed behind them.

And heard a loud ticking noise. Bending, she looked under the seat.

A square device with a timer sat there. Ticking.

A bomb.

Chapter Thirteen

Piper shouted over the storm, the engines and the wind socking the chopper. "There's a bomb under the back seat."

But Jack couldn't hear her with his headset covering his ears. She scooted back to him, knocked off his headphones and yelled again. "There's a bomb! We have two minutes before it explodes!"

"Throw it out the door," Jack instructed.

She shook her head. "It's wired to the seat's frame." Jack nodded, his face calm. "Get me my pack."

"Why?" she shouted, but he didn't answer. Instead he put his headphones back on and spoke to someone over the radio, hopefully giving their location to someone in authority. She'd read somewhere that a chopper could actually set down on the water before it sank. That might be wrong, but it gave her hope, because she didn't need a pilot's license to know that they couldn't reach land in less than two minutes.

She grabbed his pack and checked the timer. One

minute and thirty seconds. Hurrying forward, she thrust Jack's pack next to his elbow. His face full of concentration, he didn't take his gaze off his instruments.

Outside, lightning zapped through a purple sky, the thunder echoing her fears. Gusts of wind bounced off the water and buffeted the aircraft.

"Get my gun," Jack yelled.

She rifled through his pack and withdrew his weapon. Meanwhile, she could feel the chopper plunging. Her stomach swooped up her throat.

"Shoot at that boat," Jack ordered.

"Huh?" She gazed out and down through the window at the boat bobbing in the waves below.

"We've got to slow him down, or when we ditch, he'll come for us."

"You want me to shoot a boat?"

"Aim for the gas tank."

He acted as if the boat had a bull's-eye on it.

"Where's the gas tank?"

"The stern. Shoot through our windshield." He angled the chopper over the boat low and fast. "Wait. I'll get us closer."

As a police officer, she was a crack shot. Her targets were usually much smaller than a boat. But the wind-tossed chopper wasn't steady and neither was the boat battling the heavy seas. The closer that Jack could fly in, the better her chances of actually hitting her target. But she couldn't wait too long. Their chopper was about to explode.

Steady.

She aimed the gun. Tried to let her knees absorb some of the air turbulence.

Tried to strengthen her grip. But as Jack brought the chopper lower, the wind jolted and jarred them until she felt as if she was inside a roller coaster.

Jack checked his watch. "Forty-five seconds. Shoot."

She fired. Her shot resonated through the chopper and a tiny hole appeared in their windshield. A spider-web of cracks radiated from the bullet hole and wind whipped through the opening. She had no idea if she'd hit the boat, never mind the gas tank.

"Forty seconds. Empty the clip."

She kept shooting. But the only thing she knew for sure she was hitting was the windshield. More holes appeared. The plastic kept cracking. Then the force of the wind ripped the piece loose and it just missed her as it sheared off.

"Get the door open," Jack shouted, the wind whipping his words. "Thirty seconds."

She thrust an extra clip into her pocket, the gun into her jeans. Rain lashed and wind snatched at them through the open window.

Jack fought with the controls, his hands and feet working the pedals and his stick. By wedging her feet against one seat, she wrenched open the door and created a wind tunnel so strong that the gust swept her off her feet.

The chopper tilted.

She screamed, almost fell out, clawed her way back to a seat.

Jack shouted above the wind, but there was no panic in his voice. "Life jackets are under the seats."

She found them. The chopper pitched. Two bullets struck the ceiling. It took a full second for her to register that someone in the boat was shooting at them.

"Twenty seconds. Toss the life jackets out."

Jack wedged his pack into the joystick. "We're going to jump."

She looked down at the sea so far below and her stomach rolled. The massive waves stirred by the storm and the lightning flashing around them only emphasized their altitude. Wind and rain slashed at her clothes, ripped at her hair. And her gut twisted in terror. "We're too high."

"Thirty-five feet." Suddenly Jack was beside her. He grabbed her hand and the chopper rolled to one side, then another. "Ten seconds. Wait till she slides back. Then we go."

"I can't."

"Jump."

He didn't wait for her to comply. He simply dragged her out with him. And they were plunging...falling...diving...into a gray world where the water and sky were the same color.

Gray above them. Gray below them. And the only thing solid and real—Jack's hand holding hers.

Above and about two hundred yards forward, the chopper exploded into fire and burning parts.

Then she lost sight of the burning aircraft as wind clutched her clothing. Her hair slashed at her eyes. She clenched Jack's fingers and tightened every muscle in her body preparing for impact.

They slammed into the water. The waves closed over their heads. And they went down and down and down. Her lungs burned for oxygen and her eyes stung from the salt. Finally their downward momentum stopped.

She kicked hard for the surface. And all the while she kept hold of Jack's hand and he kept hold of hers.

When her head broke the surface she gasped for air, and took in a mouthful of water as a wave slapped her face. She spat out the salt, coughed, choked, finally breathed deeply. Parts of the chopper still fell from the sky, but thankfully not on top of them.

Somehow she was still holding Jack's hand. Treading water with one hand wasn't easy, but she didn't let go. Instead she kicked off her sneakers.

"You okay?" he asked.

"I'd be fine if I were a fish."

"Pretend you're a mermaid," he teased. Only Jack could joke at a time like this. "Before we went down I radioed our coordinates, but it may be a few hours until rescue arrives."

Hours? An optimistic and yet gloomy estimate.

"Finding us is going to be like searching for a needle in a haystack." And she didn't think she could keep her head above water for hours, but she didn't say so. In a critical situation like this one, staying positive was as important as inner strength.

Despite her efforts to hide her apprehension, Jack must have sensed her doubts. ''The life jackets have a radio beacon that will bring the Coast Guard right to us.''

''But we aren't wearing the jackets. You told me to toss them out.'' And in this storm, the life jackets could drift miles away from them, leading rescuers in the wrong direction.

''They aren't made to wear around the neck when jumping from that altitude.''

''Jack.''

''Yeah?''

''Do you see the life jackets anywhere?''

''No, but your shots must have hit and sunk the boat. I don't see it, either.''

She spit out another mouthful of water. ''In these waves, we can't see more than five feet in front of us. And I hate to complain...''

''You love to complain.''

''But my wet clothes weigh a ton.''

Jack grinned as he treaded water beside her. ''So take them off.''

''I thought you'd never ask.''

''But don't throw them away. We can use them for flotation until we find the life jackets.''

She wriggled out of her shirt. Not easy in the swells. ''Uh, Jack.''

''Yeah?''

"You know that boat you thought I sank?"

"Yeah."

"It's coming this way."

"DUCK UNDER," Jack ordered.

"I have a better idea," she countered as she handed him her shirt.

"What?" The boat seemed to be drifting toward them and he couldn't hear an engine, but between dips in the waves and the heavy rain and thunder, he couldn't be sure.

She ducked under the water and came up with a clip with bullets in one hand and his gun in the other. "Will this shoot when wet?"

She'd kept his gun. Cops hated to lose their weapons. But even most of them wouldn't have had the presence of mind to keep their weapon when they had to jump out of a helicopter to avoid a bomb.

"Yes, it'll still shoot, and you're amazing." Jack carefully accepted the gun and rammed the clip home. While he worked he had to let go of her hand and his feet had to churn double time to keep his neck above water.

"Change of plan."

"Okay."

He loved that she didn't argue, just trusted his judgment.

"We swim toward the boat."

She slipped off her jeans. "Do you think he's spotted us?"

"I doubt it." Jack stuffed the gun in a pocket, took her jeans and tied the cuffs in knots. Then he raised the material, swishing and trapping air in the waistband, forming a makeshift flotation device. "The chopper's explosion probably distracted him. If we're lucky, he didn't even see us jump."

"If we're lucky, we won't be eaten by a shark."

"They don't usually feed in stormy water." He handed back her jeans. "Here, hold your waistband under so the air doesn't escape, and you can rest a little while you kick."

"You call this rest?" she muttered, but she kicked and stayed right alongside him.

Jack could swim for hours. And several ex-SEALs in the Shey Group had taught him long-term flotation tricks that took little effort. He hoped they wouldn't be necessary. He'd much prefer to climb aboard the boat.

The most dangerous component would be insertion. When he climbed over the transom he would be most vulnerable to attack.

One step at a time. First they had to reach the boat undetected. While the swells helped to keep them out of sight, the huge mounds of water made swimming difficult. Although they were steadily kicking, the boat seemed to be drifting faster than they could swim.

Piper seemed to come to that conclusion the same time he did. She stopped swimming and floated on her inflated jeans. "You go ahead."

"I'm not leaving you."

"I'm slowing you down," she protested.

"Rest a minute, then we'll try again."

"I could swim faster if I lost my jeans," she muttered. But clearly she didn't want to give them up.

"How about I carry them and when you need a rest, we'll stop and refill them with air?" he suggested.

"Okay."

She didn't waste her breath arguing and he wondered how much strength she had left. She wasn't teasing or complaining. Not a good sign. And her skin was pale, her breathing strained from her efforts.

She was expending too much energy. And telling her to relax wasn't going to work.

"If we do a hard sprint, we should reach the boat. Use all your energy in one hard burst."

"Okay."

She shoved the air-filled jeans his way and started stroking for the boat. Her arms chopped the water, and she kept kicking. He tied her jeans around his waist and tried to ignore their drag.

Piper was slowly coming alongside the boat—the closer they swam to the hull, the safer they would be from being spotted. He tapped her shoulder and pointed to the stern—their best shot of climbing on board.

The boat was a cabin cruiser with dual inboard-outboard engines. The low swim deck at the stern was the easiest place to climb aboard. With the motors dead, Jack grabbed the fiberglass. The boat caught a wave and jerked him out of the water. Somehow he held on and swung himself onto the platform.

After securing a grip on a cleat, he pulled Piper up beside him. He gave her back her shirt and jeans, then removed the gun from where he'd tucked it into his slacks.

"Stay here." He spoke in a whisper.

She nodded and slipped her wet shirt over her head—not an easy task while hanging on to the rocking boat.

Jack peeked over the transom. The stern's deck was empty, except for seawater that washed over the side and sloshed into scuppers that filtered the water back into the sea. If Aaron was aboard, he was obviously holed up in the cabin where he could stay warm and dry—but not safe for much longer if Jack could take him by surprise.

The cabin had a door and windows, but the view was blocked by curtains. Good for him. Bad for Aaron.

Jack inched his way across the deck until he'd plastered his body against the windows, then tried to peer through the curtains. He saw a silhouette with a wrench in his hand, hovering over an open compartment that probably led to the engines.

With waves slamming the boat, the task of fixing a motor seemed next to impossible. Aaron should have thrown out an anchor, turned the boat into the wind to prevent it from turning sideways to the waves. If the storm worsened, the boat could roll over.

Jack wished he could throw an object to distract Aaron's attention from his entrance, but even if he could conjure a baseball out of thin air, it was unlikely Aaron would hear it strike in this wind. However, once Jack opened the door, it would be like letting a roaring lion into one's bedroom.

He had no choice.

Gun in hand, Jack kicked open the cabin door. He went in low and hard, rolling to port as the boat rocked into the trough of a wave. He skidded on the indoor-outdoor carpet and lost some skin, but ignored the pain in his shoulder.

He'd figured Aaron wouldn't be happy to see him, and he'd figured right. Aaron threw the wrench at Jack's head. He ducked, and the boat rose out of the trough, rising on the next crest and upsetting his calculation. The wrench slammed into his temple and sliced off skin. Stunned by the blow, Jack saw bursting stars, and his vision darkened. For several critical seconds he couldn't see or move his limbs. Then he found himself on his back with Aaron sitting on his chest, pummeling him with his fists.

And his numbed fingers had dropped the gun.

ON THE SWIM PLATFORM Piper finally gave up on putting on her wet jeans. More concerned over Jack's welfare than preserving her modesty, she'd watched him barge into the cabin. From her angle she'd seen nothing else. Heard nothing more.

Jack might need her help. Yet he'd told her to stay

there. He would expect her to listen…and yet…she needed to make sure he had everything under control. If she was careful, she should be able to sneak up to the banging cabin door and peek inside without him noticing her.

She edged toward the cabin. Peered inside.

Jack lay flat on his back. Too still. Unconscious? Blood gushed from a head wound. And Aaron had climbed on top of Jack. Her first reaction was to rush in to help.

She took a quick step forward. Stopped. If she could use the element of surprise to her advantage, she would be more effective.

Should she hurl herself at Aaron? She'd get only one chance. She had to make it count.

And from hand-to-hand combat drills at the police academy, she knew her strength couldn't compare to a man's. So she had to be faster, more accurate and employ impeccable timing. Her muscles tensed, ready to launch her into the cabin.

As she gathered herself, Jack shifted his hips and tossed Aaron off his chest. She pulled back. Jack was conscious. But he didn't get up. He just lay there, almost as if he was too hurt to move, and her thoughts raced.

She had to do something.

Where was the gun?

She forced her gaze from Jack to the cabin. She needed to find a weapon. Any weapon. A bloody wrench had tumbled between the stairs and a bunk, but Aaron would see her way before she could reach it.

Pillows, charts, nuts and bolts. Nothing heavy and loose. Jack groaned, yet as if his nerves had reconnected with his limbs, he sat up, blinking.

Where was his gun?

When Aaron charged again, Jack punched twice, his first blow missing as if he was a blind man trying to fight—or maybe he was just seeing double. But his second strike connected, ramming into the man's stomach. As Aaron fell on him, Jack brought up a knee into his groin, but Aaron twisted just in time to deflect Jack's blow.

Neither man had seen her.

With no weapon handy, with Jack down and Aaron's back to her, she launched her body at Aaron. Her arm went around his neck, under his chin. She tightened her hold on his throat. Fought to choke him out before he dislodged her.

Like a mangy dog flicking off a mosquito, he tried to shake her off. But she refused to be swatted, clinging as they rolled, her knee banging something hard. She gritted her teeth as fiery pain shot down her leg.

"Let go, or I'll shoot him." Aaron had found the gun, and he had it aimed at Jack.

Somehow Jack had pulled himself to his feet. Blood matted his hair and dripped into one eye. He staggered like a drunkard as he clutched a fire extinguisher.

Brandishing the fire extinguisher like a club, Jack knocked the weapon aside. Aaron's shot fired harmlessly at the ceiling before he dropped the gun with a roar of pain and anger.

Piper tightened her choke hold around his neck. And then Aaron went slack.

A trick?

No, he was out. And Jack had slid down against a bulkhead. He sat on the floor, the gun aimed at the unconscious man. "Find some line. Tie him up."

She found rope in a locker and tied Aaron's hands behind his back. She bound his feet, then tied his hands to his ankles. She wasn't taking any chances that he could free himself.

Then she turned her attention to Jack. "Let me see if I can find a first aid kit."

"No."

She paid no attention to his protest. However, the boat was rocking and rolling, and walking without holding on to a bunk or rail was impossible.

She knelt beside him. Didn't like Jack's pallor. And he'd lost a lot of blood.

And the moment she'd finished tying up Aaron, Jack had allowed the gun to drop from his hand. She reached to take his pulse. He jerked his wrist away.

He was weak, barely conscious. Yet he was still giving orders. "Get the anchor down. Radio for help."

"Okay. Okay."

The moment she agreed to do what he'd asked, he closed his eyes and slumped to the floor. She removed her T-shirt and tied it tightly around his head wound. The bleeding seemed to slow, but she couldn't take comfort in that fact. He'd lost so much blood. Too much.

The next hours were the worst ones of her life. Head wounds could be tricky. Fatal. That Jack had held on to consciousness with superhuman strength while injured gave her hope that he was now passed out due to blood loss and not a serious brain injury.

Somehow she got the anchor down. And she let out lots of line.

She ignored Aaron. Didn't try to open his briefcase. She just hoped the Shey Group would find their boat before Aaron's contacts did. If he'd been trying to meet them on the water, his contacts could be out there waiting for the storm to end.

She checked the gun. She had twelve bullets left. And a flare. It would have to be enough. She could do a lot of damage with those weapons.

And she vowed that if Aaron's contacts came, they wouldn't get his briefcase—even if she had to throw it overboard. She might not know what he had stolen, but she was prepared to defend it with her life.

She tried the radio, but either it was damaged or no one could hear her in the storm. She found blankets and wrapped them around Jack, trying to keep him warm.

He didn't look good. His breathing was shallow, his skin clammy.

She wanted to hold him, warm him with her own body heat, but she remained beside the radio, trying to make contact with the Coast Guard. No luck.

The static mocked her.

And when she finally heard an engine, she climbed onto the deck and sent up the flare. Jack needed immediate medical care. If help was out there, she needed to call attention to their location.

And if it was Aaron's friends, she tightened her hands on the weapon. Then she and Jack would die together.

Chapter Fourteen

At the sound of a baby crying, Jack opened his eyes. "Piper?"

"She's fine." A woman in doctor's scrubs hovered over him, her eyes full of concern. She lifted his eyelids and checked his pupils with a penlight.

"Where am I?" Jack craned his neck and looked around his hospital room. Piper sat sleeping in a chair, her body curled up, a blanket thrown over her.

He sat up with a frown. "I thought you said Piper was fine."

The doctor pushed him back with one hand, and Jack realized he was as weak as the baby who was still screaming in the room down the hall. And his head ached, no doubt due to the tight bandage around his forehead, which he immediately tried to shove off.

"Leave that alone, or you'll pull out the stitches my plastic surgeon sewed."

"Stitches?"

"Piper insisted you have a plastic surgeon." Logan Kincaid, wearing one of his designer suits, strode into the hospital room as if he owned the place. "Apparently she thinks you're too pretty to have a scar. And stop giving Dr. Slade a hard time."

The doctor gave an aggravated sigh of exasperation. "As if you haven't been giving me a hard time."

"I stayed out of your way."

"While you peppered me with questions. Second-guessing my diagnosis—"

"Never hurts to have a third or fourth opinion," Logan told her with the ease of an old friend ragging another. Obviously the two of them knew and respected one another. Which might have been interesting—under other circumstances.

At the sight of his boss, Jack would have relaxed, knowing he was in good hands, except that Piper hadn't moved, despite the loud discussion going on around her and the baby's screams. "What's wrong with Piper?"

"I had to sedate her," Doctor Slade muttered, "before she collapsed from exhaustion. She hasn't slept much in a week."

"A week?" Jack's eyes narrowed on Logan. "You'd better fill me in. And while you're at it, can you tell me why I'm in a...maternity ward?"

"After you passed out on the boat, we rescued you."

"Piper must have gotten the anchor down."

"She was ready to shoot us until I convinced her I was your boss."

Jack glanced at her. She looked fragile, but he imagined her pointing that gun at Logan Kincaid and he wished he'd been awake to have seen her in action. "Piper didn't want the stolen information to fall into enemy hands."

"Until we caught Aaron's friends, we thought you'd be safer here in a maternity ward."

"You caught them?"

Logan nodded as if there had never been any doubt. "The feds have them now. Aaron, too. Looks like you and Piper may have shut down a terrorist cell. You have the thanks of both the governor of Florida and your president."

Jack leaned back into the pillow with satisfaction. "I guess Piper will get her job back."

"She hasn't left your side in days."

"Days? From this little bang on the head?"

"You got an infection and fever, and with the blood loss had a hard time fighting off the infection. At first we couldn't even get Piper to change out of her wet clothes—"

Piper opened one eye. "What is it with you people—always getting women to take off their clothes?"

Then as if coming fully awake and realizing that Jack was conscious, she scrambled across the room. He expected her to throw her arms around him, kiss him. Instead she glared at him.

"What? What did I do?" Jack asked her in confusion.

"You almost died on me."

"Did not."

"You've been unconscious for days," she accused.

"Not by choice. I would much rather have been awake so you could yell at me."

Logan chuckled. "Jack, you may be a great pilot, but you really don't know much about women."

Jack pointed to the door. "If you aren't going to help," he told Logan, "you can leave now."

"But this was just getting interesting," Logan protested. Luckily for Jack, the doctor slipped her arm through Logan's and pulled him out of the room. Leaving him and Piper alone.

Jack held out his hand to her. "It's okay. You don't have to be scared anymore. I'm fine."

She ignored his hand. "You have eighty-five stitches in your head."

"You could kiss me and make it better."

"You lost so much blood. And then that infection had you feverish." Finally she walked closer and took his hand. "I didn't think you would pull through."

He didn't know what to say. So he wrapped his arms around her and tugged her close. "Did you really threaten Logan Kincaid with a gun?"

"Yeah. That boss of yours doesn't scare easy. I must have looked like a wild woman covered in your blood, but when I pointed the gun at his heart, he didn't even flinch."

Jack stroked her hair. "And how did Logan convince you he was one of the good guys?"

"He said I could keep the gun on him, but I had to let the medics get to you right away." She snuggled closer. "And that's what I did. I held the gun on him until I saw that he was going to take care of you no matter what. Then one of the team members wrapped me in a blanket and tried to force me to drink hot coffee. But I couldn't swallow. Your face was white as a death mask." She shuddered. "I've seen my share of crime scenes, but I didn't know a man could lose that much blood and live."

"You worry too much."

"We airlifted you from the ship to Tampa General. Once you stabilized, Logan brought you to this hospital and hid you in the maternity ward."

"No doubt Logan knew I'd be comfortable around all these women."

The baby in the next room finally stopped crying. She lifted her hand to his face. "Like you're in any condition to flirt. Besides, all these women are here for one reason—to give birth."

"What did you think of the babies?"

"The doc let me hold one. She thought it would be therapeutic. Give me something to think about besides you. But all I could think about was that if you died, you'd never have a child of your own. The baby made me sad. I couldn't bear to hold it."

"I'm sorry you were so worried."

"Jack."

"Yeah."

"I want us to be together."

"Okay."

"I want us to make a baby together."

"Okay. But maybe—"

She lifted her head and locked gazes with him. "Maybe what?"

"Maybe we should get married first?"

"Maybe you should tell me that you love me."

He lifted a brow, his heart light and happy. "I agreed that we could marry and make a baby and now you want more?"

"Jack, we're going to have to work on this thing you have about teasing me."

"Okay."

"Jack?"

"Okay, I love you. I adore you. Now, I just have one more thing to add."

"What?"

"You have too many clothes on."

Epilogue

Jack stood on the ground, his neck craned as he searched for a glint of silver in the clouds. The weather was clear, but with an inexperienced pilot in the cockpit, he never relaxed until after the plane was down.

With Piper at the stick, his nerves wouldn't settle. But he understood why she'd wanted her pilot's license. With as much flying as they did, she wanted to be able to take control of the aircraft—just in case anything happened to him. As if that would happen.

But he'd humored her. He couldn't help it. He loved her too much to deny her anything. Not that she asked for much. After their honeymoon she'd gone back to work on the force. He'd continued working for the Shey Group. Although the separations were difficult, the time they had together was precious and special. He'd never been happier in his life.

However, he'd be much more content after Piper landed the plane. He didn't like her going up without him. But she'd never be a great pilot without practice.

Only, now he was suffering the consequences of his

broad-minded nature. He wanted her down on the ground, next to him, in his arms where she belonged. Not up there alone.

She's a good pilot, he reassured himself. And he'd picked the plane and the mechanic himself.

After ten minutes more of waiting and no sign of the plane, impatience got the better of him. He hit the automatic dial button on his cell phone. After three rings he heard a cheery "Hi, Jack."

"You're late."

"In more ways than one."

He frowned. "What do you mean?"

"Well…"

He could hear her talking to the tower, and when she was finished, he asked, "What's your ETA?"

"Oh, that might be hard to estimate. But I figure about eight and a half months."

Eight and a half months? What the hell? And then he recalled her earlier comment about being late. And put one and one together—but one and one looked as if it added up to three. "We're pregnant?"

"Yes, Jack."

Elation and then fear struck him like a hard right to the gut. "And you're flying an airplane?"

"Well, I'm trying to, but my husband keeps phoning me every fifteen minutes to see if I've gone off course and headed to Mars."

"We're going to have a baby?"

"Yes, Jack. You'll get to be a daddy and I'll be a mommy. Does that sound good to you?"

"It would sound a lot better if you were telling me in person," he growled. A baby. They'd been hoping, trying. But he hadn't thought they would succeed so soon.

"I'll be down in five minutes."

"You feel okay? You aren't going to faint, are you?"

"Jack, I have to land the plane."

He caught the silver speck in the sky. And held his breath. She lined up for the runway with perfect precision. So why was he holding his breath? Why were his fingers clenched?

Because pregnant women shouldn't fly aircraft. Especially ones with a new pilot's license. Especially Piper.

With his heart climbing up his throat, he watched her make a perfect landing.

And before the plane taxied to a stop, he started running toward her, running toward his future. The best future he could imagine.

The phone in his hand suddenly rang and he answered. "Yeah?"

"Jack?"

"What?"

"This plane has an automatic pilot, right?"

"So?"

"So can we go back up?"

He reached the plane. "Okay. But I'm going with you."

He opened the door and climbed inside. Piper was

sitting in the pilot's seat without a stitch of clothes on. Oh, my. She was just full of surprises. And he adored every one of them.

She grinned at him. "I thought we'd celebrate our parenthood by joining the mile-high club."

He grinned. "We can join any club you want, as long as you take me with you."

"Good. Because taking you is exactly what I had in mind."

HARLEQUIN®
INTRIGUE®

presents another outstanding installment
in our bestselling series

COLORADO
CONFIDENTIAL

**By day these agents are cowboys; by night they are
specialized government operatives. Men bound by love,
loyalty and the law—they've vowed to keep their
missions and identities confidential...**

August 2003
ROCKY MOUNTAIN MAVERICK
BY GAYLE WILSON

September 2003
SPECIAL AGENT NANNY
BY LINDA O. JOHNSTON

In **October**, look for an exciting short-story collection
featuring *USA TODAY* bestselling author
JASMINE CRESSWELL

November 2003
COVERT COWBOY
BY HARPER ALLEN

December 2003
A WARRIOR'S MISSION
BY RITA HERRON

PLUS
FIND OUT HOW IT ALL BEGAN
*with three tie-in books from Harlequin Historicals,
starting January 2004*

Available at your favorite retail outlet.

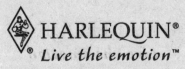

HARLEQUIN®
Live the emotion™

Visit us at www.eHarlequin.com

HICCAST

"Georgette Heyer has given me great pleasure over the years in my reading, and rereading, of her stories."
—#1 *New York Times* bestselling author Nora Roberts

Experience the wit, charm
and irresistible characters of

GEORGETTE HEYER

creator of the modern Regency romance genre

Enjoy six new collector's editions with forewords
by some of today's bestselling romance authors:
**Catherine Coulter, Kay Hooper, Stella Cameron,
Diana Palmer, Stephanie Laurens and Linda Howard.**

The Grand Sophy
March

The Foundling
April

Arabella
May

The Black Moth
June

These Old Shades
July

Devil's Cub
August

Available at your favorite retail outlet.

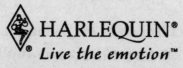

HARLEQUIN®
Live the emotion™

Visit us at www.eHarlequin.com

PHGH

eHARLEQUIN.com

Sit back, relax and enhance your romance
with our great magazine reading!

- **Sex and Romance!** Like your romance
  hot? Then you'll *love* the sensual reading
  in this area.

- **Quizzes!** Curious about your lovestyle?
  His commitment to you? Get the
  answers here!

- **Romantic Guides and Features!**
  Unravel the mysteries of love with
  informative articles and advice!

- **Fun Games!** Play to your heart's content....

**Plus...romantic recipes,
top ten lists,
Lovescopes...and more!**

**Enjoy our online magazine today—
visit www.eHarlequin.com!**

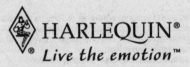